Falling
for the
Player

Falling for the Player

JESSICA LEE

Entangled Publishing, LLC
2614 South Timberline Road
Suite 109
Fort Collins, CO 80525
Visit our website at www.entangledpublishing.com.

Embrace is an imprint of Entangled Publishing, LLC.

Edited by Alycia Tornetta
Cover design by Letitia Hasser
Cover art from Shutterstock

Manufactured in the United States of America

First Edition January 2017

embrace

For my one and only. I can't imagine my life without you.

Chapter One

Getting laid by a hot guy—now that's something I can get behind.

Pun totally intended. Maximo Segreti smiled to himself.

However, sharing that juicy bit of info with his best friend Abbie Donovan would only result in him being set up on a string of dates with every gay man she knew in a twenty-mile radius. Mentally, he rolled his eyes at the thought. *God, no.*

"Come on, Max," Abbie groaned. "For once in your life, let go and live a little."

Lowering his glass of Coke onto the scratched surface of the bar, Maximo Segreti sighed. "I *am* living, Abbie." Going on a pub crawl with a dozen of his not-so-closest friends wasn't his idea of time well spent. He knew his friend wanted him to have what she thought of as "fun," but drinking until he ended up on his knees praying to the porcelain god... Thanks, but no thanks.

"It's a pub crawl, not a caravan across the Mexican border."

"You asked me to come out to Charlie's, not hit every bar

around here. Besides, I may be a junior, but you know I'm not even close to twenty-one yet."

"Max… You'd be with us. We'd find a way around that little problem." She pouted, her bottom lip making its full appearance for maximum effect. Shit. He kind of felt bad for the man who finally succumbed to her charms and ended up her husband. She was hard as hell to say no to. "It'll be so much fun!"

He shook his head, refusing to be sucked in this time. "Staying right here and finishing my Coke will be all the fun I need. Besides, I have a paper due Monday. I can't afford to blow the rest of my night drinking and end up feeling like shit tomorrow."

"Jesus!" Abbie rolled her eyes. "You are such a nerd sometimes." She cupped his face, a smirk lifting the corner of her mouth. "But you're too freaking cute for me not to still love you." She laughed and planted a kiss on his cheek.

"Get outta here," he said.

"Laters." She turned to leave.

"Don't do anything I wouldn't do."

She paused and glanced back over her shoulder, her long, cinnamon curls swaying across her back as she lifted one dark brow. "Seriously?"

"Just saying…"

"I'll try to keep that in mind." She chuckled and blended into the small group leaving.

Max still couldn't believe he'd allowed Abbie to convince him to come out when he still had so much work to finish. Sure, he imagined that for most college students a pub crawl would be a blast, if a guy didn't have to stay in the top one percent of his class so he'd be accepted into law school. He'd never done anything at an easy pace. He'd graduated high school at seventeen so he could get a head start at college. That way, law school would be within his reach even sooner.

For as long as he could remember, it had been his and his father's dream that Max follow in his father's footsteps to become a partner at the Segreti Law Firm, and they were determined he'd make that a reality sooner rather than later.

"Sometimes sacrifices have to be made, son, when it comes to taking care of what matters most." His father's voice rattled around inside his head, and his fist tightened around the cool glass. Nothing mattered more than family and the firm. And to the Segretis, they were one and the same.

"Hey, can I get a Bud Light?" a deep male voice called out from beside Max. A guy plopped onto the vacant stool, shoving his fingers into the dark auburn waves of his hair, pushing them back over his forehead with a heavy sigh.

"Bad night?" The words popped out before Max could curb his curiosity. He wasn't exactly an extrovert, but even in his peripheral vision, he could tell the other man's body language spelled misery.

"Yeah." The guy nodded and snagged the fresh bottle of brew, quickly downing a large swallow. "Try 'bad week.'"

He glanced Max's way, and recognition slammed into him along with a wave of lust that arrowed straight to his groin. He repositioned himself on the stool.

Holy hell. It was the Gamecocks' notorious running back, Patrick Guinness.

"Wow," Max managed to force out through the desert he'd once called a throat. He grabbed another swig of his drink before adding, "Sorry, man."

"Me, too," Patrick grunted, but his hazel gaze, hooded by lashes thicker than any man should have the right to claim, never strayed from Max, as if he were trying to size up how much further he should take their conversation. Reaching over, he stuck out his hand. "I'm Patrick."

Shit. He's actually introducing himself.

"Max." He slid his fingers into Patrick's grip, and the

player's calloused palm grazed Max's sensitive one, firing off a weird fluttering sensation inside his midsection. *What the fuck?* Max didn't get flustered. But damn if that wasn't precisely what sitting next to Mr. Tall, Red, and Hot-as-hell had done to him.

He'd seen Patrick on campus and television. Everyone knew who PG was, although the nickname was quite ironic considering his X-rated reputation. The guy was known to be a badass player on and off the field. He was the University of South Carolina's star athlete, while Max, according to Abbie, was a nerd with his head stuck inside a book, meaning he and the running back didn't exactly move in the same circles. So he'd never met Patrick in person.

Up close… The guy was good-looking on the TV, but less than a foot away? Patrick made him forget how to breathe. At over six feet tall, with shoulders that plowed a football across the field, he consumed the space between them. He had full lips, a square jaw, and sexy dimples that were created for a man to kiss and lick. Max's mouth watered, and his pants tightened from the fantasy building inside his head.

In other words, Patrick possessed a face Max was sure melted all the girl's panties.

He'd give his left nut for the guy to be gay.

Clearing his throat, Max cocked his head. "You're Patrick Guinness, right?"

"Oh, you recognized me, huh?"

"I doubt you'd find a person in a fifty-mile radius who doesn't know who you are." Max smiled. "Sorry about last weekend's game."

"Yeah." Patrick took another pull off his beer.

"I didn't see the whole thing, but I did catch the final score."

"We got our asses kicked," Patrick said, lowering his bottle. The longneck hit the bar's surface, the thick glass making a *clunk* on the wood. "Not our best game."

"Damn. That had to be tough."

"Hey, can I get another here?" Patrick called out to the bartender and held up his Bud, his bicep bulging under his short sleeve. The veins in his forearm stood out in sharp relief under the glow of the bar's neon signs, a clue to the number of hours Patrick had to spend in the gym lifting. An image formed in Max's mind of Patrick straddling a bench, flat on his back, sweat beading on his arms, his face, running a trail down his throat and onto his chest as he heaved the weighted bar. Over and over again he grunted, thrusting the heavy burden high until he cried out with exhaustion.

Damn!

Max sighed. What he wouldn't give to be held down beneath all that restrained power…a euphoric rush. His gaze roamed Patrick's loose black T-shirt, which covered his chest, hiding a narrow waist and flat stomach. Based on the size of his arms, Max knew Patrick's abs had to look like a damn topographic map of the Blue Ridge foothills.

Getting fucked by Patrick Guinness would leave a man bruised and sore, marked like prey claimed by a predator. And it would be amazing. The muscle behind Max's sternum knotted then kicked hard. His pulse surged, and the room tilted, driving him to seize the edge of the bar and steady himself. Christ. He'd never daydreamed about shit like that before. Sex? Sure, like any other guy he had his late-night moments, his fantasies for when he needed a release. But this was different. Max surveyed the athlete casually sipping on his next beer, and another spark of heat went straight to his balls, tightening them. PG was different.

"You have no idea," Patrick added, glancing in Max's direction. "I don't mean to be rude, but fuck, can we talk about something else besides football?"

"Shit." Max scrubbed a hand over his face, trying to clear

his head. "Yeah. No problem."

"Tonight, I just want to drink and forget." The corner of Patrick's mouth quirked, and it had to be the sexiest damn thing Max had ever seen in his life.

Max lifted his glass in Patrick's direction. "Here's to forgetting." Their glasses clinked, and Max took another sip of his soda as the football player knocked out his second beer.

"So tell me, Blue Eyes," Patrick said. "What are you trying not to think about?"

You. Max bit his tongue to keep the word from slipping out.

Patrick's gaze roamed from the top of Max's head downward in a way that had his pulse jumping back into high gear. That's when it dawned on him. *Blue Eyes?* The endearment looped inside his head. *Patrick couldn't be…?* Max had seen him with girls. But of course, that didn't mean he couldn't be bisexual.

Mentally shaking the thought away in favor of a safer subject, Max proceeded to inform PG that he was a junior prelaw student with plans to join the family firm.

"No pressure to escape there." Patrick snorted and motioned to the bartender to bring him another.

"True." Max sighed. "But honestly, I can't imagine doing anything else." And that was the truth. Even though his father had been grooming him to follow in his footsteps since the day he'd been born, he found the field of law interesting and exciting.

"Either way." The football jock shook his head. "Law… that's fucking hard, man."

"I can't deny that." Max lifted his glass and waved it at the room. "It's why you wouldn't normally see me here."

After taking a long pull of his fresh beer, Patrick grinned. "Then I guess it's my lucky night." He leaned in, allowing his bottle to clink against Max's tumbler.

The flirtatious gleam in Patrick's eyes sent a wave of lust barreling through Max's veins. The mouthful of Coke he'd intended to swallow suddenly lodged in his throat, cutting off his air. He coughed, somehow still managing to coerce the liquid down his esophagus without spewing it across the bar.

Patrick's large palm landed between his shoulder blades. "You okay, dude?"

Trying to recover his voice and not think about the heavy feel of the hand on his back, Max nodded. Maybe PG was drunk? But he was only on his third beer. Could such a big guy be that much of a lightweight? Not likely, given the hard-partying reputation of the football players. So, was PG actually flirting with him? His pulse raced at the heady prospect.

Think about it, dude. A jock and a book nerd getting it on?

No way could this be happening.

And there went his rational mind, slapping him back from his quick trip to fantasyland. The damn thing was such a cockblocker.

The fact that he hadn't gotten laid in more months than he cared to think about probably had his imagination working overtime.

"Yeah. I'm fine," Max finally said. "I don't know what went wrong there."

"Shit happens, man." Patrick returned to his drink, his fingers easily wrapping around the bottle and then some. Max couldn't stop an image from forming in his mind of that same hand curling around the running back's thick shaft, his fingertips straining to connect around the circumference. *Oh, yeah.* What he wouldn't give to taste him. Ride him.

Max swallowed a groan. If the heavenly Father was kind and just, He'd blessed the ripped player with a dick in proportion to the rest of him. At least that was Max's prayer.

Geez…who prays about the size of another guy's cock?

I'm going to hell for that one.

"Don't worry about it."

Max's erection throbbed once more behind his zipper, and he eased a little farther beneath the bar's overhang to better block the view of his lap. Time to change the subject.

"Not that I'm complaining, but why aren't you commiserating with the rest of your team?" Something about the tight hold Patrick had on his drink, and the strain around his eyes, said there was a lot more going on with him than the loss of one game.

"That's exactly why I'm here and they're wherever the hell they decided to hang," Patrick said. "I just needed to be somewhere else. Clear my head. Got a lot on my mind, you know?" He sighed, and then stabbed his fingers through his hair again, pushing it back. That move needed to be illegal. "Like I said, I don't want to talk football."

And that was fine with Max. He was more than happy to sit next to the hottest guy on campus and chat about whatever the hell he cared to, for however long he wanted. So for next couple of hours, they rehashed the entire last season of *Grimm* and *Elementary,* then engaged in a heated debate on when and if the producers should allow Joan and Sherlock to hook up. Patrick, of course, was a rabid supporter of Sherlock "tapping that" as soon as possible, while Max felt that if they allowed them to become a couple it would change the whole chemistry of the show.

"No, dude," Patrick groaned. "You got it all wrong. Don't you realize that the only reason everyone is still watching is for the moment those two finally get naked?"

"Or at least for a shot of Sherlock's bare ass," Max blurted out. *Oh, shit!* He closed his eyes, his pulse a ticking bomb inside his head. "Did I say that out loud?"

"Yes, you did," Patrick said, and the deep, masculine vibration of the three words licked up Max's spine.

He glanced over at the redhead, apprehension coiled like

a spring in his chest.

"Are you gay, Max?" Patrick had his elbow on the bar with his Bud dangling between his fingers.

"Yeah," he said, his heart stuttering. Everyone in Max's circle knew he was gay. He didn't make a habit of hiding who he was from his friends, and he wasn't about to start now. So why the hell was he shaking on the inside? "Does it matter?" Max snagged his Coke from the counter, more to do something with his hands than because he needed a drink.

"Only if I wanted to hook you up with a girl." A sly grin formed on the player's mouth. "But why the hell would I want to do that?" Patrick's eyes narrowed on him, his hazel gaze wicked, as if taunting him for a response.

What the hell is going on?

"I have no idea?" Max whispered and shook his head. Gooseflesh lifted every hair on his arms, and the urge to two-fist the other guy's shirt, pull him in, and crush his mouth with his own hit him hard. Instead, he gripped his glass harder and stared at the ice swirling around in the caramel-colored liquid. Throwing caution to the wind had never been his style. Besides, there was no way that someone like Patrick was into him. No way. Right?

"This was really great," Patrick said. "I mean that. But I should head home before I end up wanting to take a hammer to my head in the morning." Straightening from his stool, he pulled out his wallet and plopped some cash on the bar.

"How are you getting home?" Max stood.

"Uber." Patrick tapped the screen of his cell.

"You don't need to do that. I can be your designated driver." He had no idea what the fuck he was doing, offering to drive Patrick home. All he knew was he wasn't ready for the night to end. Not until he understood what had just happened between them.

"You don't even know where I live." Patrick stared down

at him, the corner of his mouth quirking up.

"I bet if you gave me the address, I could manage to get you there." Max grinned. Shit. Patrick was too damn hot when he smiled like that. And he was about to drive him home.

"You're a nice dude, Max. I can tell you're smart." Patrick nodded. "You're going to make a great lawyer."

"Thank you." He chuckled. Funny how intoxicated people always got the urge to spout revelations and predictions about others. "Now, let's go." Max led the way to his Jeep Cherokee.

"An SUV," Patrick said, rounding the hood toward the passenger side. "How very civilized and…domestic of you, Segreti."

Max couldn't help noticing how steadily Patrick managed to maneuver across the gravel parking lot, despite the half dozen beers the guy had in his bloodstream. The athlete's mouth might be loose, but he seemed to be in complete control of his senses. Max clicked the remote, unlocking the doors. "Bite me, Guinness."

They slid into their seats and the doors banged shut.

Patrick turned to face Max, pinning him with heated scrutiny. "Would you like it if I did?"

Max's throat tightened, and the world collapsed inward, leaving just the two of them. The rapid beat of his heart filled his ears. How the hell was he supposed to answer that question? What did Patrick want him to say? *God, yes! You can bite me anywhere you want. Or, hell no! You're kidding me, right?*

"You're drunk, PG," fell out of his mouth instead. Max shoved the key into the ignition and the engine roared to life.

Chicken! I'm a complete chicken. The hottest guy I've ever met is flirting with me and I brushed it off!

"Yeah." Patrick barked out a laugh, grabbed his seat belt, and repositioned in his seat. "I got my buzz on. And you have no idea how good it felt to just…not think for a little while."

That was where he was wrong. Max had a very good idea how that would feel. It would be sheer bliss. But he couldn't afford that luxury. He had to be on his toes, keep everything in perfect order. In fact, if he were honest, the thought of letting go kind of scared the hell out of him.

After getting directions from Patrick, Max backed out of his space and pulled onto the road. He glanced across the car at the hot-as-hell player with his head tossed back against the headrest, eyes closed. Max's studied the curve of his throat, the fine dusting of hair peeking out of the V of his T-shirt. Hell, even the way his Adam's apple bobbed was sexy.

Damn it, he wasn't ready for this to be it. Everything about Patrick tempted Max to step out of his comfort zone. For once in his life, do something totally unscripted. Odds were they would never see each other again. Hanging out at a bar with PG was one of those rare, once in a lifetime moments. This could be a night he'd never forget, or he could drive Patrick to his apartment and always wonder if he might have said yes. Not that he thought they'd actually hook up. But damn, it'd be sweet to hang out with him one-on-one for a little while longer. What did he really have to lose?

"Hey, you know, we could go back to my place," he said, the words tumbling out of his mouth before he could chicken out. From the corner of his eye, he watched as Patrick turned his head toward him. Max risked a glance, silently praying for a positive reaction.

"Your place?"

Well, it wasn't a no.

"Yeah." He shrugged. "I could make some coffee, and we could watch something on TV. You know, hang out some more before I drive you home."

A grin brightened Patrick's expression. "That sounds like a plan," he said. "My head's still pretty clear, and I could go for some vegging out in front the tube. My roommates are probably still out getting wasted." He huffed.

"So, we're heading to my place, then?"

"Sure," Patrick said. "Why not?"

"Great," Max replied, keeping a tight hold on his excitement, though his hands trembled with restraint. A fact he hoped like hell Patrick didn't notice.

"Will your roommates mind me coming over this late?"

"I have my own place." For a moment, Max cut his eyes from the road.

Patrick's head rolled to the side again, facing him. "That must be nice."

Max nodded. "It'll just be us."

"Cool."

Holy shit. Patrick Guinness is coming home with me.

The rest of the twenty-minute ride passed in silence while Patrick appeared to study the passing scenery as if lost in thought. Max pulled into the open parking space in front of the black and cream-colored stucco condo building his father had purchased. With each unit possessing over two thousand square feet of living space, the place had more room than he needed. But never let it be said that the Segretis ever did anything in a small way.

Max turned off the ignition. "We're here."

Patrick grabbed the lever to his door. "Nice looking place."

"Thanks." Max exited the car.

Patrick joined him and they climbed the wrought iron staircase to the second story. Max made short work of the deadbolt and let them in. He flipped the switch beside the entrance, and a couple of lamps as well as an overhead chandelier illuminated the open floor plan.

"Damn," Patrick said. "This place is fucking huge." He eased forward and down the one step landing into the den. "It's really just you here?"

"Just me." Max sighed and dropped his keys on the granite counter separating the kitchen from the living space. "I can focus and study easier in the peace and quiet. So I decided to live here instead of the dorms."

"Makes sense, if you can afford it," Patrick said.

"I'll get some coffee brewing." Max rounded the smooth stone edge of the black and white island. "The TV remote should be on the coffee table," he called out from the kitchen. "I'm fine with whatever you want to watch."

It didn't take long before the sound of gunshots ricocheted off the walls followed by the high pitch screams of a woman who apparently wasn't ready for whatever was about to happen.

Two coffee pods later, Max had their mugs filled with some steaming Colombian brew. Coming from the kitchen, he found Patrick kicked back on the cream-colored, L-shaped sectional, his black-denim-clad legs crossed and his booted heels propped on the table. One arm rested on the back of the sofa, and the short sleeve of his graphic T-shirt revealed a bulging bicep and the jagged edges of a tattoo. *Oh, hell yes.* Max cleared his throat, making a mental note to somehow get a closer look at that ink. "Cream or sugar?"

"Oh, neither," Patrick said. "Thanks."

After loading his own dark roast up with a few spoonfuls of sugar and a hefty dose of cream, he made his way to the sectional. Patrick accepted his cup, and Max sat down near Patrick's end of the sofa.

"*The Avengers*," Patrick said. "Good with you?"

"Sure." Max nodded. "I've seen it at least five times, but I love it."

"Yeah?" Patrick chuckled and took a sip of his coffee. "Me, too."

Halfway through the movie, Max still couldn't get over how easily he and Patrick had clicked. Who would have thought the football player was funny? He was so different than Max would have thought. Instead of being conceited or stuck up, Patrick was laid-back and really down to earth. And it wasn't just the alcohol, because even though Patrick had several beers at Charlie's, Max didn't believe he had been that wasted. Max surveyed the redhead, whose attention was locked on the fifty-inch flat screen as he balanced his mug on his chest. The tension around his eyes had eased, and for some reason seeing Patrick relaxed, knowing he may have had something to do with that, felt good.

"The draft will be here in a matter of months," Patrick said, breaking the silence between them. "It's my junior year, but there's a good chance I'll be a first-round pick. No time like the present, you know?"

"Really?" Max placed his cup on the end table, the statement catching him off guard, especially since Patrick hadn't wanted to discuss the sport. "That has to be exciting."

Patrick's hand fell to his knee, his long fingers working the kneecap through a well-placed rip as if he were trying to soothe an ache. "The NFL is what I've worked for, trained for, for what feels like forever. It's do-or-die time, Max. For me and my family."

"You got this, PG. And I can't blame you. You're too damn good not to make it."

Patrick rested his elbows on his torn jeans before settling his cup on the table. "You're good for my ego, Blue Eyes." Patrick shot him a lazy smile, and Max's cock jerked at the sight.

"I'm gonna make us some more coffee." Max stood and grabbed his mug. He had to get out of there before he did something he might regret...like jumping Patrick, straddling his hips, and riding the man like he was a stallion who'd inhaled his first breath of freedom.

"Sure." Patrick leaned back, allowing him to pass and to

snag his mug along the way.

In the kitchen, Max closed his eyes and regrouped before heading back to the den with refills.

"Here you go," Max handed over a cup. Patrick blindly reached up at the same moment Max realized it was the wrong mug and started to switch.

But it was too late.

The redhead's large hand hit the ceramic bottom, tipping the hot contents directly onto his chest.

Chapter Two

"Fuck!" Jumping up, Patrick yanked his soaked shirt over his head.

Damn, that shit is hot!

"Oh, fuck!" Max grabbed the wet shirt and tried to soak up the remaining coffee dripping off Patrick's skin. "God, this is my fault. I should have been more careful." Then Max jerked his own T-shirt off and blotted Patrick's chest with it, his expression twisted with concern. "Are you okay?"

He was fine. Not that Max would stand still and listen long enough to find out. Fuck, the guy was too adorable. Patrick was lucky the coffee had been Max's heavily creamed version and so not hot enough to do any damage.

Patrick braced his hands on the other guy's shoulders, trying to hold him in place, but it wasn't working. "Max," he called out to him.

"Do we need to get you to the ER?"

"I'm fine."

"Shit, Patrick, I—"

Seizing one of Max's wrists, Patrick hauled him against

his chest, bringing a halt to whatever else he'd been about to say. Max looked up, his eyes wide, stunned.

"I'm okay," Patrick whispered. He couldn't stop drinking in the other man's features. Strands of Max's dark hair had fallen forward onto his forehead. The guy had the most expressive dark blue eyes, with small flecks of amber around the pupil he hadn't noticed until now. Patrick followed the bridge of the man's perfectly straight nose lower to where it ended above the carved V of his mouth. Outside of his looks, Max was everything Patrick never went for, smart and obviously rich, judging by the expensive car and his big-ass condo. Back home, the only way he and Max's type would have mixed would have been when he worked on their cars. Funny how his popularity as a football star placed him, for once, on the other side of the tracks. Someone who would soon be rolling in the big bucks. The pink tip of Max's tongue appeared, momentarily short-circuiting Patrick's train of thought as Max licked his full lower lip.

Fuck.

Patrick wasn't sure who moved first, but the next thing he knew, he had his fist clenched in Max's short, thick hair and his lips sealed against Max's. A hard shudder of pleasure raced over him, and Patrick's cock bucked against the confines of his zipper. Max groaned, his mouth roaming every inch of Patrick's mouth, as if he couldn't get enough. But Patrick matched his every move, unsure who needed the contact, the pleasure, more.

"Damn," Max breathed. "That was nice."

"Yeah. It was." Loosening his grip, Patrick cupped the back of Max's head, savoring the silky texture of his hair.

"Then why the hell are we talking?" Max latched onto Patrick's shoulders, drawing him closer. It was all the encouragement he needed.

He slammed his mouth back onto the sexy nerd's. Teeth

clicking, they went at each other in another hungry kiss. Fuck, he wanted Max. He'd had more women than he could keep track of since starting at USC, but none of them made him forget like Max did. Made him not care about his fucked up knee, the next game—about anything other than getting Max beneath him, grinding into him until neither one of them gave a shit about their next breath.

Trailing his hands down Max's back, Patrick located his target. *Hell, yes.* He squeezed the firm, round globes and rocked into Max's hips, grazing their erections against each other with the sweetest of pressure. Max groaned against Patrick's lips, and the sound was the hottest damn thing he'd ever heard.

None of this made any sense. It wasn't like he'd never been with men before. It had just been a while. Not because he'd been hiding the fact he was bisexual—he simply hadn't found any guy that had interested him enough. Until now. And from what he could tell so far, Max wasn't even into sports. *What the fuck?* But dammit, something about Max had crawled under his skin and heated his blood. And hell if he could ignore it any longer.

"Tell me you want me to fuck you," Patrick demanded against the other man's lips, maneuvering him backward until Max bumped the wall.

Releasing a moan, Max scattered hot, open-mouth kisses along Patrick's jawline as his fingers found and hooked the waistband of Patrick's jeans. His hands slid around to the front until he reached the zipper. "I want you," Max rasped.

Patrick clasped Max's wrists, halting him. "Say it," he insisted, his tone gruff. He needed to hear it. Needed to know that Max wanted him as desperately as he did him. But more importantly, he needed to know if Max would give him control, something he didn't have over most of the shit in his life. But he needed it tonight, if only for a little while.

Max's glared, and he jerked his arms as if testing the strength of Patrick's hold. What came next, though, caught Patrick by surprise. The corners of Max's mouth lifted with the hint of a smile. "I want you to fuck me."

A haze of lust nearly blinded him, and he dragged in a ragged breath. Releasing his hold, Patrick flipped Max around. "Put your hands on the counter."

Max obeyed.

"Good," he said. "Now, don't move."

"Okay," Max breathed.

Reaching around, Patrick unbuttoned the other guy's jeans and slid the zipper down. Max groaned, widening his stance.

"That's right." Patrick ran one hand under Max's shirt, enjoying the warm, hard feel of the guy's flat abs. *Mmm…* He worked the fingers of his other hand beneath the denim. "You want me touch you, don't you, Blue Eyes?"

"Yes," Max said, and his head dropped lower. "Do it."

Patrick ran the blunt tips of his fingers beneath the waistband of Max's briefs, so fucking close to the guy's shaft, but not nearly close enough. His own cock throbbed with anticipation. His heart raced, thumping against his breastbone. He swallowed hard, forcing moisture down his throat.

"Do what?" Patrick pressed his chest against the other man's back. "I want to fucking hear you say it," he rasped.

"Touch me." The breath shuddered from Max's lungs. "Fuck. I want you to touch me."

"Damn." The word rumbled from his chest. "That's hot." Patrick groaned and slid his palm farther beneath the band. Heat enveloped his hand right before the smooth, hard flesh of the other guy's cock nudged his fingertips. Max hissed. Patrick wrapped his fingers around it, working the rigid shaft upward, freeing the crown. Fucking hell, he was hung. Sliding his thumb through the slit, he smoothed a drop of pre-cum over the sensitive tip. Patrick's mouth watered.

"Fuck," Max bit out and rocked his hips.

"I totally agree." He stroked the pulsing shaft. "I have to taste that."

"Shit, yeah…"

Releasing his hold, he grabbed the waistband of Max's jeans and briefs and shoved them to the floor. Patrick smoothed his palms over the man's bare ass. Damn, his flesh was perfect. Golden. Smooth. Firm.

Unable to wait another second to feel Max against him, Patrick quickly opened his fly and pushed his jeans down past his hips. He hadn't bothered with briefs before he'd headed out, so his cock sprang forward, rigid and glistening. Easing closer, he worked his shaft between Max's cheeks and rocked, sliding his erection upward and back within the clasp of his buttocks. *Oh, hell yeah.* The pleasure was just too fucking sweet, and he couldn't have forced the groan back down his throat if he'd tried. The sound filled his ears.

"Patrick," Max groaned and squirmed. "You feel…"

He pressed Max's cheeks tighter against his shaft, savoring the friction, the heat. But it wasn't enough. His fingertips dug into the man's hips, and his jaw ticked. The desire to bury himself inside Max soared to a fevered pitch.

"Damn, Blue Eyes." Patrick ripped his hands away and forced himself to step back. "Turn around," he rasped, wanting to taste the hot nerd's cock before he lost control.

Max did as instructed, shoving his jeans across the floor as he rotated, facing Patrick. Air rushed in and out of his partner, and his blue irises were hazy with lust. His cock jutted and flexed toward his navel. Thick veins traveled the sides of the shaft, ending at a flared, darker crown.

Dropping to his knees, Patrick wrapped his fingers around Max's stiff rod and glanced up.

Max groaned, locking his gaze with Patrick's. "Don't stop."

"No fucking way." Patrick edged forward, flattening his tongue on the backside of Max's cock. Licking upward, he didn't slow down until he touched the sensitive zone beneath the lip of the crown. Max hissed and shoved his fingers into Patrick's hair, tugging on the roots.

Yeah, you like that.

Patrick engulfed the head, continuing to work his tongue, teasing the bundle of nerves. He pumped the shaft, spiraling up and down in time with the suction he applied to the tip.

"Damn," Max gasped. "Gonna make me come." Despite the sound of objection in his words, Max rocked his hips, thrusting his cock hard into Patrick's waiting mouth. That was fine with him. He was dying to taste everything the guy had to offer.

Once more, he followed the vein up the backside of Max's cock with his tongue. Max moaned, and his head lolled.

"Love that," he whispered.

Patrick traced the crown, dipping into the slit for another sample of the salty pre-cum before swallowing his lover's shaft.

"Fuck!" Max yanked at Patrick's hair, and the head of his cock bumped the back of his throat. Patrick hollowed his cheeks and swallowed, taking him deeper.

"Goddamn…" Max's breath hitched. "I'm coming. Fuck…coming." He clawed at Patrick's scalp, but the sting went straight to Patrick's own cock. A wave of hot fluid hit the back of his throat. Even though it had been a couple of years since he'd last been with a guy, he thought he was prepared, but the volume caught him off guard. He coughed and convulsively swallowed, but he didn't lose his hold. He continued to work the length, spiraling up and down. Jet after jet of cum erupted from the tip, spilling from his lips and over his hands. Damn, Max was hotter than fuck. And Patrick was determined to lap up every delicious drop.

"Jesus," Max said, his voice rusty. He nudged Patrick's head and pulled free. "That was..." Max shook his head, panting. "Damn, you're kind of good at that."

Patrick wiped the corners of his mouth with thumb and forefinger and smirked. "Thanks." He straightened to his full height. Cupping the other guy's nape, he pulled Max against his chest. "Just wait until I show you some of my other talents."

He crushed his mouth onto Max's, his blood too hot for him to wait for an invitation. Max opened as if the fierceness of Patrick's need fed his own. Patrick dove inside, demonstrating with his tongue exactly what he'd meant by his words. A low groan welled from the back of Max's throat. Christ, he loved how Max seemed to crave it as hard as Patrick needed to give it. With previous lovers, he'd always felt like he needed to hold back.

Breaking away, Patrick clasped Max's face. "Please tell me you have condoms and lube in this place."

"We're in luck." Max smiled and glanced toward the back of the condo. "Come with me." He latched onto Patrick's wrist.

"Oh, I plan to do just that." He grinned. That was going to be the easy part. Letting go of the sexy nerd when the sun came up...now that was an entirely different issue. But his family, his future...it all lay in the hands of the upcoming draft.

So letting go was exactly what he'd have to do.

Chapter Three

Three years later

Not much had changed in Columbia, South Carolina, since Max had been gone, including the weather.

July was still hot as hell.

Tapping his blinker, he turned his BMW convertible into the parking lot of Guinness Tire and Wheel Alignment and parked in front of one of the garage doors. Damn. He dreaded leaving the cool interior of his vehicle. But after driving cross-country to return home from grad school a couple of months ago, he really needed to get his car checked out.

Glancing up at the sign mounted over the office, he mentally rolled the name of the business around in his head. Flashes of the night he'd shared with a certain Guinness raced across his mind's eye—the running back on his knees, deep-throating Max's cock as he erupted with an orgasm so intense his brain nearly short-circuited; Patrick above him, holding his legs back and pounding into him over and over again.

Max had never been able to eradicate that night from his

mind. No matter how many men had come and gone from his bed, he'd always found them wanting. But sex hadn't been the only connection between them, despite the fact that it had been mind-blowing. He liked to believe that something more than a physical attraction had occurred that night. At least, he'd felt it, and he was sure Patrick had to have sensed it as well. When Patrick had walked out to his waiting Uber that morning his good-bye had been curt, but the look in his eyes hadn't been nearly as cool as his tone.

"I had fun, but…you know, football has to come first. I don't have room for a relationship in my life. Maybe I'll see you around sometime?"

But they never did. The draft had been coming up, and Patrick had had to keep his focus on the end game. The last thing he'd needed was some guy trying to cling to him. Besides, he'd had his own career goals to focus on.

He shook his head. Still, he'd never been able to let the memory of that night go.

He opened his car door and stood, then shrugged free from his blazer and tossed it on the seat. He had to admit, even though the shop came with great reviews, the name probably had more to do with why he'd selected the business. His college one-night stand had been a USC Gamecock, so odds were good that Patrick could be related to the owner. Not that he would be hanging around, since the Packers had drafted him shortly after their night together. After Patrick signed, Max had kept his head in his studies, forcing himself not to follow the guy on the internet or TV. If he had, he might have never made it in to—or through—law school. Besides, what would have been the point? He knew that night had been a hit-and-run.

Patrick had made it to the big time.

And I was just a blip on the guy's radar along the way. So why can't I forget?

Making his way into the office, Max looked over the well-worn surroundings. The place was clean, but the furnishings were tattered and the walls were definitely in need of a coat of paint.

He stepped up to the counter, and a tall, lean guy wearing a navy T-shirt turned to greet him.

"Good morning," he said. "What can we help you with today?" He shoved back a thick strand of dirty-blond hair from his eyes.

"Hi." Max braced his hands on the edge of the counter. "I was hoping someone could work me in for an alignment and check my tires."

"Sure," he said. "We can fit you in. Can I get your name and the info on your car?"

Max filled him in on the details. "By the way," he began, his stomach tensing in anticipation of his next words. "I was wondering if the owners might be related to Patrick Guinness?" *What are you doing?* "You know, the running back for the Packers, who used to play for the Gamecocks?"

What did it matter? If the answer was yes, what was he going to do with the info, leave a note for Patrick like some sort of lovesick schoolboy?

"Yep…" The blond grinned, showing off an unexpectedly perfect set of white teeth. "You got the right place. Did you go to USC?"

Holy shit!

"I did." Max couldn't help but smile in return. The guy had an infectious personality. "Met him once, too, and when I saw the name of the place, I had to ask if this was the same Guinness family." *Shut the hell up, Segreti! Are you going to tell him you fucked him once, too?*

"Hang on a minute." He walked over to a door that looked like it led to the shop and pushed it open, stepping halfway over the threshold. "Hey, Patrick! Someone's asking for you."

"He's here today?" Max managed to spew the three words despite the state of shock his brain cells were in.

"Sure is." The blond looked back at him. "He runs the place."

Oh no. No, no, no. Max's heart stuttered, and his fists tightened until he held the laminated surface of the counter in a white-knuckle death grip. *He's here? What the fuck? I thought he was with the Packers?*

What in the hell was a person supposed to say to their one-night stand when they ran into them years later? What was Patrick going to think?

Stalker, much?

No. Max shook himself. He was overreacting. It wasn't like this was the following week, and he was hanging in the hallway after every one of the guy's classes. *Chill out, dude.* This was perfectly normal. Slowly, he released his death grip on the counter. This was a chance encounter.

A few moments later, a familiar, deep voice sounded on the other side of the door. "What did you say, Tommie?"

"I said someone is asking for you."

"Oh, okay." The door jingled, and Max braced himself. "What's his name?" Patrick rounded the corner.

"Max Segreti."

Over six feet of pure muscle ground to a halt, and Max's gaze locked with Patrick's.

Holy hell.

It shouldn't be possible. But the former football player was even better looking than Max remembered. A mass of auburn waves covered his head in an "I just crawled out of bed, but I don't give a shit" manner. Yet somehow it made him look even hotter. Max swallowed hard past the dry lump in his throat.

Even though Patrick wasn't on the field any longer, his

arms had remained ripped. They just looked more like the kind of muscle maintained by hard work instead of hours beefing up in the gym. His dark blue T-shirt stretched over his upper body, the cotton pulled taut across his pecs, doing its best to contain his build.

Max's gaze dropped, taking in the guy's narrow waist, and farther down to where his legs were encased in a pair of rugged blue jeans. The denim hugged thighs built for power. And damn if Max didn't remember all too well the strength the other man possessed. The way he could pound a man until he saw fucking stars yet still begged for more. His cock stirred, threatening to embarrass him if he didn't take his mind elsewhere, fast.

"Max," Patrick said, yanking him out of his fantasy. The big guy strode forward and up to the counter. He stuck out his hand, as if he were saying hello to an old study-group buddy instead of a former lover. *Damn.* A twinge of disappointment arrowed into his midsection. What had he expected, though? A kiss? Considering how many people Patrick had probably slept with since their night together, it was amazing he even remembered Max. "It's been a while."

Max slid his palm into the other guy's, and despite the cool greeting, the calloused palm sent shockwaves of heightened awareness along his nerve endings. Blood rushed to his cock, taking him to an immediate rock-hard state. *Shit. One handshake. What the hell, Segreti?*

Thank God for the high counter.

Max pulled his hand free. Had Patrick felt it, too? Shoving his hand in his pocket, he risked another glance at Patrick. Cool. Collected. If he had felt anything, the guy was damn good at keeping his reactions tightly reined.

"Yeah, it's been a while," Max said, finally finding his voice.

"How did you two meet?" Tommie propped an arm on

Patrick's shoulder. Max had never been more envious of an extremity in his entire life.

"We ran into each other at a bar one night, and he kept me company while I proceeded to get hammered." Patrick chuckled.

"Oh, damn! You had to deal with Guinness wasted."

"Hey!" Patrick shoved at Tommie's arm. "I can handle my alcohol."

"He wasn't that bad," Max added. "In fact, the way I remember it, we both had a pretty good time that night." Yeah. That wasn't subtle at all, but he couldn't stop himself from throwing those words out there to see if Patrick would give anything away. Anything that said he remembered just how good a night they'd had.

Slowly, Patrick turned his head, his hazel eyes finding Max's. Maybe it was his imagination, but Max could swear the green flecks in Patrick's irises burned a little brighter. Oh, yeah. He remembered all right.

"So this is the first time y'all have seen each other since?" Tommie tucked a pen behind his ear and propped a hip on one of the desks behind the counter.

Eyes narrowed, Patrick glanced over his shoulder at the dirty-blond. "Don't you have something you should be doing?"

"Oh." Tommie straightened. "Oh, sure." He stepped forward and swiped Max's key fob from the counter. "I'll get your Beamer pulled in and assessed." Grinning, he nodded and quickly made his exit.

The room spiraled into a heavy silence, the weight of it nearly suffocating.

"He seems like a nice guy," Max said. It was either that or turn and run for air.

"Yep." Patrick nodded. "Tommie's been with the shop for six years. He's the best."

"Great staff can be hard to find."

"You finish that law degree?" Patrick pointedly looked at Max's dress shirt and slacks.

"Yeah." Max smiled, unable to contain the thrill that he'd remembered the small detail of him studying pre-law. "I graduated in May."

"Good for you." Patrick snagged a pen off the counter, working it between his fingers. "I'm sure your father is proud."

"What about you? I'm kind of surprised to run into you here. Last I heard you were with the Packers."

A flash of what Max could only describe as pain washed over the guy's expression, but it was there and gone so fast, Max wasn't sure he'd seen it at all.

"Long story," Patrick grunted. "Bottom line: shitty luck and a bad knee. Both landed me back home."

"Damn." His heart hurt for what Patrick had lost. He could only imagine how difficult it would be to have the one thing you'd worked toward your entire life ripped away. He could relate. If, by some twist of fate, he failed to pass the bar… He didn't even want to think about it, because he had no idea where he'd go from there. "I hadn't heard." He shook his head. "I am so sorry. I know how much football meant to you."

Before he could think better of the move, Max reached out and grasped Patrick's hand. Maybe it was his imagination—or wishful thinking—but he could have sworn he heard Patrick's breath hitch.

"Yo, Pat!"

As if the sound of his name were a wakeup call, Patrick blinked and yanked his hand away. Max curled his fingers into a fist and dropped his arm to his side. God, what he would have given for a few more minutes to hold on to him, to savor the feel of his skin next to his.

The shop's door banged and a replica of a younger Patrick

came through and plopped down onto one of the task chairs. In a move just like his brother, the teenager drove his fingers through his hair and shoved it out of his eyes. Where Patrick's hair was auburn, the kid's was a deeper brown, and it brushed his shoulders.

"Yo, Liam," Patrick mocked. "What's up?"

"I just wanted to tell you that I'm spending the weekend with Kyle."

"I thought you and I had plans to hang out?" Patrick crossed his arms, and Max tried to avoid staring at his bulging biceps.

"Things changed." Liam shrugged. "What do you want me to say?"

"Nothing." Patrick shook his head. "I don't expect you to say anything." Sighing, he turned his attention back to Max. "Max, meet my not-so-little-anymore brother, Liam. Liam, this is Max, a friend from USC."

"Hey there. Are you a football player like your brother?" Max asked, doing his best to lighten the tension in the room.

Liam lifted his hand in sort of a half-ass "you're not actually going to make me speak to you, are you?" wave. The sight was too comical to be offensive. *Teenagers.* Had he ever been that much of an asshole at that age? He'd probably spent too many hours studying to ever be so rude.

"Yep," Liam said. But apparently that was as much as he was willing to offer on the subject.

"Sorry," Patrick muttered. "There once was a time he possessed a few manners."

"Bite me," Liam said, but the words lacked any venom.

"Seriously, brat?" Patrick hit him with a glare.

"Don't worry about it." Max chuckled. "I have a younger sister. So, you run this place with your dad?"

"Dad's dead," Liam stated. His tone was flat, yet somehow the words dripped with pain.

"Oh." Max looked up at Patrick, but the former NFL player was staring at the counter and his clenched fists. "I didn't realize. I'm sorry for your loss." Max glanced over at Liam, but the younger Guinness picked at his fingernails, acting as if the other two men in the room didn't exist. As if he weren't bothered by the fact that his dad was gone. He reminded Max of an injured animal licking his wound, trying to make himself feel better. And failing miserably.

Thanks to Max.

He'd been there less than half an hour, but he had somehow managed to bring up not one but *two* painful and uncomfortable subjects.

"It's okay," Patrick said, his words somber. "He passed away last year."

"Kyle will be picking me in a few, and I need something to drink." Liam pushed from his chair and marched from the office. Christ. Could Max feel like more of a prick for opening his big mouth?

"I really am sorry." His gut churned. Patrick had to still be grieving not only the loss of his career but his father. A hell of a lot to handle in such a short time. "If there's anything I can do—"

"There's not," Patrick said, cutting him off.

"Okay." Max nodded.

"What are you doing here, Max?" Patrick braced his hands wide on the counter. "You show up in your expensive car and business suit, bringing up the past. What is it you really want from me?"

Max blinked. *Where the fuck did that come from?* "I'm here to get my car aligned. You are in the business of alignments, correct? Or is there something else you offer that I'm not aware of?" He didn't enjoy being a smartass. But when pushed, he could give as good as he got. He'd learned from the best. His father didn't get to be the head of a law firm by always being a perfect Southern gentleman.

Patrick glared, and his jaw ticked.

"All right, Mr. Segreti," Tommie called out as he came through the door.

Patrick squared his shoulders and backed away from the counter, making room for the other man.

"We've got your BMW ready for you," Tommie said. "The alignment was off, so it's a good thing you brought it in before you started to wear your tires. They still look good, by the way. You have plenty of tread left."

The blond dropped the key fob and the invoice in front of him, but Max barely registered what else the man said. He couldn't shake Patrick's reaction. He'd acted as if Max had shown up knowing he worked there, looking for a quick and dirty fuck. He couldn't deny that the attraction for the guy still burned, but if he was interested in a hookup, those were easy to find.

Max pulled out his wallet, tugged his credit card free, and handed it to Tommie. "Thanks for getting me in so quickly."

"No problem." Patrick rested his backside against the corner desk, his arms still crossed. "We're happy to be of service."

Tommie handed over Max's card and receipt. "Thank you for your business, Mr. Segreti. Don't be a stranger."

The heat of Patrick's gaze burned into Max as he answered, "Thanks, Tommie."

The service tech murmured something to Patrick about another job in the shop and headed back out, leaving Max alone once more with the former player. He cleared his throat, and not wanting things to end tense, he pulled one of his cards free.

"Look," Max began. "I honestly didn't know you were in town or that this was your family's business. But I won't lie and say that it wasn't a pleasant surprise." Max eased closer and set his business card on the surface between them. "I'm back in town now, for good. I wouldn't hate it if you called me sometime."

Patrick's expression, once again, was unreadable. Then he lifted the card.

"Segreti Law Firm." Patrick looked up from under his lashes. "Living the dream, huh?"

"If the dream comes with a lot of paperwork and hours of studying for the bar, then yeah, I'm living the hell out of one." He laughed, hoping to lighten the mood between them.

Patrick slowly nodded. "I'm happy for you, man."

"Thank you," Max said. "Again, I really am sorry about earlier, if I upset you or your brother."

"Don't worry about it."

"Okay, then. I guess I should be heading back. My lunch break is probably long over." Max stepped away.

"Why do you want me to call you?"

He stopped dead in his tracks. His mind whirled from the absurdity of the question. "Why wouldn't I?"

"Me and you…" Patrick shook his head. "I'm sure your father would just love the idea of you hanging out with some has-been with grease under his nails."

Squaring his shoulders, Max locked eyes with Patrick. "I may be a Segreti, but I make my own decisions. Especially when it comes to my social life."

"Wow…times *have* changed, then." Patrick smiled, and the effect was devastating. So much so, Max barely registered the rest of his sentence. "The nerd has a social life now."

"Is that you trying to be funny?" Max lifted a brow. "So you're a comedian now, too." He grinned. "Good one."

"Hey…" Patrick shrugged, lifting his palms. "I'm multitalented."

"I wouldn't go that far." He laughed, but quickly sobered. Anticipation, nerves, and who knew what else had climbed into his stomach and turned it inside out. No one else ever made him feel this way. The last time he'd been this shaken was the night he'd first met Mr. Hot-As-Hell.

Would Patrick call? Or would he toss his number in the trash? Shit. Max needed to just get the hell out of there before he made any more of a fool of himself. "Anyway. Like I said. I should go." He backed away and headed for the exit.

"Hey, Max," Patrick called out, stopping him at the threshold. "It was really good to see you again." The corner of the redhead's mouth lifted in a carnal half smile. One that resembled the same look Patrick had given him after swallowing his cum.

Fuck. Now how was he supposed to think about anything else for the rest of the day? Or, hell, ever again.

Chapter Four

"So…how *close* were you and this Max guy?"

Coffee spewed from Patrick's mouth, splattering the stack of papers on his desk.

"Liam!" Patrick spun his chair around and faced his younger brother, who stood in the shop's doorway, his arms crossed. He'd closed a few minutes ago, and he'd thought everyone had gone home for the day.

"I know you. He was more than a *friend*, wasn't he*?*"

"Where do you come up with this shit?" He turned back to the massacre that had once been the day's invoices.

"I'm just stating the obvious." Liam strolled farther into the office and made himself comfortable on top of the counter, his long legs swinging but barely missing the floor. Damn. The kid was going to be taller than Patrick if he didn't stop growing soon.

"What are you still doing here, anyway?" He gathered a handful of paper towels from a roll on the shelf behind him and did his best to wipe away the coffee. "I thought you left an hour ago. Weren't you going to hang with your friend?"

"I did, but he has to go to his dad's for dinner. He's going to pick me up later. I knew you'd still be here, since you have no life."

"I have a life," Patrick gritted out.

"Like Max?"

"You don't know a damned thing." *Ignore him and he'll go away.* Isn't that what they always say about pesky little brothers? He shoved the invoices back together, attempting to get them into a neat stack.

"So, you and he haven't…?"

"Damn, Liam!"

He rolled his eyes. "What? You're not denying it."

"Leave it alone, kid," Patrick groaned.

Liam jumped down from the counter. "I was right. I knew it the moment I walked in on you two. The way you were looking at him."

"Stop! Stop!" Patrick slapped his palms over his ears. "You're going to make my brain bleed."

He stared at the numbers on the paper, trying to remember what the hell he was doing. Not discussing his former love life with his brother, that was for sure. Since Patrick had become Liam's guardian, he'd always made sure that if he required a release, his brother was nowhere around. He never wanted Liam to be affected by his sex life.

"What is this, anyway?" Patrick slapped the stack of papers onto his desk. "Are you writing an essay about my love life?"

Liam dragged the chair away from the other desk and rolled it up to the front of Patrick's. With his palms up in mock surrender, Liam added, "I'm just making an observation."

"Maybe you should consider applying some of these skills in school and not just on the field."

"Kiss my ass."

"Not in a million years."

His brother would be a senior in the fall, and it dawned on Patrick that the kid's hormones had to be firing on all cylinders. Even before Liam had come out to him and their dad, Patrick had known his little brother was gay. The world was a different place, more accepting, but being gay in high school still wasn't easy. Especially being an out high school football player in the South. Patrick intimately understood how hard that road was to travel. The question and answer session had to be more about how he'd hooked up with Max rather than a sudden interest in Patrick himself.

Patrick went on to tell Liam that he and Max had met at a bar one night. His mind drifted back to three years ago when he'd slid onto the stool next to Max's. The guy had looked up at him with those big blue eyes and that crooked smile with its lone, fuck-me dimple, and *bam*! He and his other head had been more than "into" him.

He looked up and saw his brother staring at him, waiting for the slightest hint that Patrick was still into Max. Oh, hell no. Was there anything more awkward than talking to one's younger brother about one's sex life? "That was a long time ago, and neither one of us had been interested in anything more," he said, hoping he'd put an end to his brother's curiosity.

"He smelled like money," Liam said, his nose crinkling as if he'd gotten a whiff of something bad.

"And your nose would be correct." Patrick shoved the invoices in his desk drawer. He'd total the small batch of tickets in the morning. He didn't have the energy for it this evening. With his desk cleared, he spotted the card Max had given him and picked it up. "You ever heard of Segreti Law Firm?"

"Maybe? I think I've seen some of their commercials on TV."

"That's his family's firm," Patrick said.

"He leave you his number?"

"Yep."

"You planning on calling him?"

Patrick glanced once more at the bold black digits. He had to admit, he'd never forgotten that night, and no one had ever come close to getting under his skin like Max had in those few hours. Even though Max had known who he was, he hadn't treated him any differently because of it. He'd been down-to-earth, perfectly happy to drink coffee, talk, and watch TV together. He'd been hot—still was, dammit—but not too into himself. Max's dark brown hair was a little longer than he'd remembered it, but he still kept it short and off his shoulders. He also appeared bigger than when he'd been at USC, like he'd been working out and lifting weights at the gym. He bet the guy looked even more delicious out of his expensive clothes.

Patrick surveyed his immediate surroundings—the dust clinging to his desk, the grease and dirt smeared on his knuckles and under his nails. They would never work. Not back then, and definitely not now. He flicked the card into the trash bin next to him. "Nope," he said. "I'm not calling him. We wouldn't have a damn thing in common, anyway."

A bark of a laugh came from his brother. "Good. You two together would have been weird. You deserve better than to be some rich guy's boy toy."

"What do you know about being a boy toy?" It was strange hearing those words come out of his younger brother's mouth, but it wasn't something that hadn't already crossed Patrick's mind. Max seemed like a decent guy, but men from his social circle didn't usually look for partners in Patrick's economic class unless they wanted a temporary walk on the wild side.

"Jesus, Pat." Liam rolled his eyes. "I'm almost eighteen. Give me some credit."

Patrick shook his head. "It freaks me out when you talk like that. But thanks, I think, for caring."

"If you ever repeat how *caring* I am to anyone, I'll punch you in the throat."

Laughing, Patrick said, "Yeah, right. Only if you want to get your ass kicked."

"You don't think I can take you?" Liam pushed his chair back, slung his leg over, and stood. He shoved the short sleeve of his T-shirt a little higher, flexing his bicep.

"Oh, shit," Patrick said, doing his best not to lose it. Liam had definitely been working out, and it showed. But Patrick had him beat in size by at least forty pounds. "Look at that… that thing. Damn, I'm scared." He pretended to shake.

"Shut up." Liam dropped his arm, but not before letting him know exactly how he felt with the flip of his middle finger.

"No, dude, seriously." Patrick sobered. "I can tell you've been hitting the weights."

He shrugged. "What else do I have going on right now besides school?"

Patrick sighed. But before he could say anything else, a car horn blew, drawing their attention.

"That must be your ride," Patrick said.

"I'm out of here." Liam headed for the door.

"Stay out of trouble!" Patrick stood and grabbed his own keys. He was so done. All he cared about handling for the night was a cold beer.

"Yeah. Yeah," Liam called out. "Don't worry. I'll be fine."

He did worry. He'd always worry, because his brother deserved someone who cared enough to be concerned about what happened to him.

And because "I'll be fine" weren't famous last words for no reason.

• • •

Four hours later, Patrick took another swig off his bottle, his head finally reaching the perfect buzz he'd been chasing. He lowered the empty glass onto the bar's stone surface.

"Buy you another?"

Patrick glanced over at the guy who'd slid onto the stool next to him. Late twenties. Maybe thirty. Dark hair. Dark eyes. Full mouth. And the perfect five o'clock shadow every guy wished they could grow.

Nice. Very nice.

Club Proclivity always drew the best-looking crowd, which was one of the main reasons why he'd never cancelled his card. That and the fact that the private fetish establishment had offered him a free membership the first time he'd visited, when he'd been with the Packers. Why hurt their feelings and throw away a good thing in the process? Proclivity gave him a place to find what he needed without any strings, and without having to parade his one-night stands through the house in front of Liam. Plus, it didn't hurt that the club was located about twenty-five miles outside of town, far enough away to keep whatever he did after work his own business.

The stranger leaned in closer, connecting his gaze with Patrick's. "Or is there something you see that you'd prefer instead?"

"You don't waste any time, do you?"

"We're all here for one thing." He shrugged. "Why play games? Well, unless that's your thing." He smiled, displaying a perfect set of white teeth. "If so, I've been known to be fun once or twice."

Of that, Patrick had no doubt.

"Then I suggest we find a table, Mr. Fun." Patrick stood without looking back and headed for one of the darkened booths near the rear of the club. This was exactly what he needed to take his mind off today, and off certain people from his past who were never going to be a part of his present—or his future.

He slid onto the leather and moved toward the center of the half circle. Mr. Fun entered from the other side and edged around until his thigh brushed Patrick's. Palming the other guy's nape, Patrick yanked him closer, crushing his mouth onto the man's. Mr. Fun moaned into the kiss and opened. Patrick thrust his tongue inside, tangling with the other guy's. The flavor of the club's best bourbon washed over his taste buds. Hot. Bitter. Nothing like the sweet taste of coffee and cream he remembered. Shit.

Not now. Focus.

The stranger broke away on a gasp. "Damn, you kiss as good as you look." Mr. Fun's hand slid over the crotch of Patrick's jeans. "I bet you taste just as nice, too."

His pulse should have been pounding. The guy was fucking hot. His hand was doing its best to give his cock a wake-up call. Yet…

Nothing.

Dammit.

Since when had he ever not been able to lose himself in a beer and an anonymous fuck?

"Hey, baby," Mr. Fun said. "Where'd you go?" He cupped his face, turning Patrick's attention back to him. Max's face flashed inside his mind. *"I want you to fuck me."*

Patrick's cock swelled, kicking the air from his lungs. He gasped. "What did you say?"

"I said I want you to fuck me." The dark-haired stranger squeezed Patrick's awakening erection, shooting a bolt of sensation through him. And not in a good way. Patrick mentally cringed. "You like that idea?" the other guy asked. "I'll see if they have a room."

Oh fuck, no.

Mr. Fun started to pull away, and Patrick grabbed his arm. "Hang on," he said, as his phone began to vibrate in his pocket. *Thank God.*

"Problem?" The other guy eased back down onto the seat.

"I have to take this." Patrick exited the booth and tugged his cell from his jeans. Sliding his finger across the glass, he moved toward the front of the club, distancing himself from the music as he lifted the phone to his ear. "Hello?"

"Mr. Guinness, this is the Sheriff's Department. I'm calling about your brother, Liam."

The officer's words hit him in the chest with enough power to stun his heart.

Battling through the fog of shock, he managed to force his throat to work. "What's happened?"

. . .

After the world's longest Uber ride ever, Patrick slammed the shop's door behind him and set the deadbolt. There wasn't any use in going home. No way in hell he was sleeping tonight, not when his brother was in *jail*. He groaned at the thought of Liam behind bars.

Inside the office, he plopped onto the task chair behind his desk and dropped his head into his hands. This couldn't be happening. His brother arrested for possession of marijuana. What the hell had he been thinking, messing around with weed—not to mention mouthing off at a cop? Did he want to blow any chance of getting a football scholarship?

Fuck it.

He slammed his fist onto his desk, the heavy thud resounding in the hollow space of the room. Liam was a damn good football player, too. Probably even better than Patrick had been back in high school. Not that he'd ever tell his brother that and risk it going to his head.

How was he supposed to handle this?

"God, I wish you were here right now, Dad," Patrick

whispered into the shadows. "If you were, Liam wouldn't be acting so damn erratic. He's lost, floundering without you, and I'm a shitty substitute for a father figure." He scrubbed a palm over his face, the scent of Mr. Fun's expensive cologne still lingering on his skin. He squeezed his eyes shut and shook his head. "How am I supposed to help him grow up, get his head on straight, when I'm not even sure half the time what I'm doing with my own life?"

Sighing, he turned on the computer and logged into their personal banking account to check the balance.

"Shit." Liam's bail would drain the majority of what was in their account. Plus, Liam was going to need an attorney. Where the hell would they find the funds to pay for everything? Someone who would work hard to make sure his brother's future was protected. He sure as hell didn't want to leave Liam's case in the hands of a public defender.

Out of the corner of his eye, the white business card lying on top of the pile of discarded papers in the trash caught his attention. He snagged the simple yet elegantly embossed card from the bin.

"Maximo Segreti." He whispered, yet the name reverberated inside his skull, the effect hijacking his pulse and sending it into overdrive.

He should stay away from the guy and not risk the temptation of starting something when it would lead nowhere except straight to a crash and burn. But at the moment, Max was the only tie he had to someone in the legal field. And even though that connection had simply been a one-night stand, something told him he could trust the guy when it came to his brother.

Curling his fingers around the card, Patrick swiped his keys from his desk with his other hand. With some sort of plan in place, he could go home and wait for the sun to rise.

Chapter Five

Elbowing open the glass door, Max trekked through the employee back entrance into Segreti Law Firm. He slid his arms into his gray sport coat and straightened his tie as he rounded the corner into the first floor main reception.

"Good morning, Max," Abbie said from her desk, which faced the waiting area, where a bulletproof shield separated her from their clients and visitors.

"Good morning," he said. "It's beautiful outside today, isn't it?" He grabbed his chair, plopped down, and dragged over a stack of files one of the partners had asked him to research. It was tedious work, but after yesterday's surprise of running into Patrick again… Yeah. Things just felt better.

"Well, someone's in a good mood." Heels clicked on the hardwood floors and approached his back. "What gives, Max?"

He glanced over his shoulder at his friend. After college, Abbie had quickly jumped into marriage. But it had ended after only a year when she'd caught her husband in their bed with her best friend. Max had still been in grad school, but when she'd moved back home and needed a job, he had put in a good word for her with his father. "I don't know what you're talking about?"

"Oh, please." She tsked. "I haven't seen you with a smile like this in weeks. All I've seen is the back of your head because you've either had your nose in a book studying for the bar, or been absorbed in a stack of paperwork."

"I've been busy."

"I know. But I also know something's different this morning, so spill. You know you want to." She braced her hands on her hips. "What's got you so happy?"

Abbie had been his best friend since their freshmen year at USC, and when she got like this, he knew there was no use trying to avoid giving her something. She wouldn't stop. But he loved her anyway. He knew no matter what, she would always have his back.

"Fine," he said, giving in. "I ran into someone yesterday that I hadn't seen in a really long time."

"Ohhh…" Her expression brightened, her brown eyes growing wide. She tossed her long, cinnamon-colored hair over her shoulder and parked her backside against his desk, facing him. "You mean like a someone you knew intimately kind of someone?"

"Possibly." Max flipped open one of the folders, hoping that would be enough to appease his friend.

"Oh my God," she whispered, her voice dropping lower. "Who? Was it somebody I knew and you never shared the details, despite the fact I told you everything?" She slapped his arm.

Nope. Not enough by a long shot.

"What happened with him was over before it ever began." He shrugged.

"But you liked him." She bent closer, smiling. "You liked him a lot."

"Maybe." He grasped a pen from his desk, flipping it end over end, doing his best not to grin in return. Just because he and Patrick had run into each other again didn't mean anything. They took a short trip down memory lane yesterday, and more than likely it would end there.

"So, who is this guy? Are you going to see him again?"

"I'd rather not say for now. And I don't know." He turned his attention back to his work. "Probably not."

"Oh my God," she groaned, her voice hushed. "You're killing me." Noise coming from the front window interrupted them, and Addie hurried to her desk.

At that same moment, his cell vibrated inside his blazer. Max pulled it out and checked the display. The number wasn't one that he recognized. Curious, he answered.

"Hello?"

"Max?"

"Yes."

"Hi, Max." The caller cleared his throat. "This is Patrick. Patrick Guinness."

Holy shit. As if he needed the guy's full name.

"Hi," he finally said, finding his voice. "You caught me off guard. I wasn't expecting to hear from you so soon." *Shit.* Internally, he cringed. That came out wrong. "Not that it's a bad thing. I'm glad you called." *Damn. Damn. Damn.* He was babbling. "What's going on?"

"I was wondering…" The line went silent for the longest two seconds of Max's life. His pulse throbbing in his throat, he leaned over his desk, waiting. "I was wondering if you were free for dinner tonight?"

Is he asking me out?

He swallowed hard, searching for the moisture that had abandoned his mouth.

"Dinner?" He grabbed his pen and worked the plunger up and down under his thumb. "Sure. I haven't made any plans." *Yes!*

"There's something I need to talk to you about."

Something in Patrick's voice sounded off. "Okay," Max said. "Is everything all right?"

"My brother, Liam… You met him yesterday." There was a brief pause, as if he were searching for the right words before he continued. "There's been some trouble, and I could use your advice."

"Oh…" Disappointment parked its heavy ass on his chest. Patrick hadn't called to ask him for a date. He wanted to talk about a legal issue. "This is sort of a business meeting, then."

"In a way, yeah," Patrick said. "You stopping by and leaving your card yesterday turned out to be perfect timing. I hope you don't mind, but I kind of need your help."

Patrick Guinness needs my help. The concept looped inside his head.

"No. That's no problem at all," Max found himself saying. Not that turning him down was even on his horizon. At least he'd get to spend a little more time with the former jock. "I'm happy to help."

"Thank you. It's just something I'd rather not get into over the phone."

"Sure," Max said. "I can understand that."

They agreed to meet at one of Max's favorite Italian restaurants, Bella's, at around eight. It had a very cozy, family atmosphere, so it shouldn't feel like an intimate date.

Max ended the call, but he couldn't tear himself away from the phone's screen. He was going to see him again. Tonight. His grip tightened on his cell as images of Patrick on his knees, swallowing his cock, ran through his mind. So beautiful. So hot. His shaft responded, swelling, aching behind his zipper. Damn. Not here. Yet he was helpless to stop the replay.

Why couldn't he get the guy out of his head?

"Was that him?"

Abbie's voice caught him by surprise, and his cell clattered onto the hard surface of his desk. He snatched it up and stuffed it back inside his pocket. "What are you doing? Working on your mercenary skills, and sneaking up on a person is next on your list?"

"I'll take that as a yes." She flashed him a cat-that-caught-the-canary grin. He frowned. "Chill out. I didn't overhear all of your conversation. Only the last part where you agreed to meet him for dinner. So you're seeing him again." She winked.

He groaned. "It's not what you think. He has some legal questions he wants to ask me."

"Oh." Her expression morphed from one of victory to empathy. "Well, you're still having dinner. Just because you may be discussing business doesn't mean that this couldn't turn into something more later."

"You are an eternal optimist, woman."

"It's part of my charm." She laughed, and Max couldn't help but join in. "And part of why you love me. You need me to help balance your scale."

"Oh, because I'm such a pessimist? Since when?"

"Since we're talking about the men in your life," she said. "You never give them a chance. You're always so sure it's not going to work out."

"That's because none of them have been—"

"Been…?" She planted a palm on his desk, leaning in as if to hear him better.

Shit. He couldn't believe he'd almost spilled Patrick's name.

"Nothing." He slapped one of the folders closed, grabbed two of them, and stood. "Besides, you know how my father feels about me being gay," he said, keeping his voice low. "He's fine with it as long as I keep my love life under wraps and not in his face or in front of the media. So why should I put a lot of energy or optimism into any relationship?"

He knew his father loved him, but there were times when he felt the firm meant more to him than his own family. His mom, on the other hand, lived for Max and his younger sister, Teresa. But it was their father who set the tone in their home, and part of that meant Max keeping his private life utterly private. He didn't like it. This was the twenty-first century, after all. But so far there hadn't been much to keep quiet about. So to keep his father happy, he didn't discuss anything with him outside of school or work.

Sighing, he glanced down at the material in his hand. "I need to get these back to Tom."

"Right." She returned to her desk. "I'm here for you, Max. Anytime. Don't forget that."

"I know," he said and made his way down the hall. But there wasn't anything Abbie or anyone else could do that would change his father's opinion, or his expectations for his son. Max's life had always revolved around seeking his father's approval, making him proud. He didn't know how to live any other way.

• • •

Later that evening, Max sat in a corner booth at Bella's. The position gave him a clear view of the front door so he could spot Patrick when he entered. He was early. But being on time was one of his pet peeves. He couldn't tolerate the idea of being late. It drove him a bit crazy.

Maximo "Control-freak" Segreti.

"That's me," he whispered to the empty booth.

But he had to be. He had to keep a firm grip on everything in his life or else it—his life, his career, his plans—could fall apart. And as a Segreti, chaos wasn't tolerated.

Tightening his fingers around his Coke, he savored the

cold feel of the glass. The temperature contrast helped to ground him, gave him something to focus on besides waiting for the door to swing open.

He took a sip of his soda. At that moment, the wooden door swung open and Patrick strode over the threshold. Max couldn't tear his gaze away. Patrick didn't enter a room. His mere presence dominated it, claimed the space around him. He was only a year older than Max, yet he carried himself like a man who'd seen many more years. Confident.

Strong.

No one would ever suspect the number of losses he'd suffered.

But Max knew. And he respected Patrick even more for how he'd been able to move forward, running his family's business and taking care of his younger brother. Patrick may have lost his contract with the NFL and his star status, but in Max's eyes, he was as amazing as ever—if not more so. And despite the rebellion inside his head telling him this was a bad idea, he couldn't deny that he wanted Patrick. Maybe then he could burn his memory out of his head, and he could move on.

Max beckoned Patrick with a wave, and he headed over. His heart galloped in his chest at the sight. Patrick's long strides quickly carried him across the dining room. He'd dressed in a forest green polo and a pair of dark jeans that Max would have sworn Patrick had been the mold for, judging by the way they hugged his thighs and cupped his ass. Perfect. Max inhaled deeply.

This is going to be the longest business *dinner ever.*

"Hey there," Patrick said, sliding onto the seat across from Max. "Thanks for meeting me on such short notice."

"Hi." Max smiled. "No problem. I'm glad you called." And that was the God's honest truth.

Before they could continue their conversation, their

server appeared, a rotund older gentleman everyone called Pops. "What can I get you, son?"

"I'd love a beer," Patrick said, glancing up. "Do you have Bud Light?"

"We do." Pops nodded and wrote the order on his pad. "How about an appetizer for you two?" He grinned. "We've got the finest fried mozzarella in town."

"No, thanks." Patrick picked up the menu from the table and started flipping through the pages.

"Nothing for me," Max said. "Thanks, though, Pops."

"Okay. I'll be right back with your beer."

Max turned his attention to Patrick, who was reading over the menu.

"You're still a fan of Bud Light, I see."

Patrick looked up. "You'd think I'd be sick of the shit after all the gallons I've consumed over the last three or four years. But nah." He shoved a few auburn waves off his forehead. "It's still my go-to beer." He nodded toward Max's soda. "And you're still serving as the designated driver, I see."

"I never acquired a taste for alcohol." Max shrugged. "But that's fine with me. I prefer keeping my head clear and staying in control."

"Really?" Patrick's brow lifted. "That's not exactly how I remember you."

Heat bloomed in Max's neck and traveled north. "That was different."

"Here you go," Pops announced, and Max wasn't sure whether to be grateful or pissed as hell at the interruption. Pops placed Patrick's beer in front of him. "You boys decided on what you'd like to eat yet?"

"I'll have the lasagna," Max said, going with the first thing that came to mind. It wasn't as if he were hungry anyway. Not for food, that was, with Patrick sitting across the table from him.

"Make that two," Patrick added, handing Pops his menu. Max did the same, and their server quickly jotted down their orders.

"All right. Two lasagnas." Pops nodded. "We'll have that out to you shortly," he said before leaving.

"So," Max began. "You said there's been some trouble. What can I do to help?"

Patrick placed his forearms on the marred oak surface of the table. "It's my brother." He lifted one hand and dragged a weary palm over his face. "He was arrested last night for drug possession. I bailed him out this afternoon."

"Damn." Max shook his head. "I'm really sorry, man."

"These last two years have been hard on him with losing our dad. Our mom died from breast cancer not long after Liam was born. And our father was never close to what few extended relatives he had. So our dad was everything to Liam."

"He's still got you," Max said.

Shaking his head, Patrick said, "I don't know how much that means."

"Don't sell yourself short. You have more to offer him than you realize."

"Right now, I'm not so sure." He sighed. "I just had to bail my baby brother out of jail. So I don't think I'm winning any prizes for my parenting skills."

"Kids have a mind of their own. Or don't you remember?" Smiling, Max took a sip of his Coke. "It wasn't that long ago we were teenagers. Despite the greatest parental advice in the world, kids will rebel. Test their boundaries."

Patrick huffed. "Well, his rebellion could cost him his future."

"What can I do to help?"

Their dinner arrived, and over the next hour while they ate, Patrick informed him of his brother's desire to play college football like him, but how, with an arrest on his record, this could damage his career.

"After the loss of my NFL contract, and my dad's illness, we don't have much left when it comes to our finances," Patrick went on to say. "But I'll do whatever it takes to make sure my brother has a good attorney. That's why I called you."

"I don't sit for the bar until later this month. But…" Max sat back against the booth's cushion. "Our firm has some of the best attorneys in the state. I can see who is available and get you a meeting."

"That would be great." Patrick rotated the bottle between his fingers, glancing up at Max. "It would mean a lot. I can't stand the thought of a stupid mistake screwing up his entire future."

"I totally get it," Max said. "I'm sure we can help him as long as he's committed to keeping his nose clean going forward."

"Oh, he will be, or I'll bust it for him," Patrick chewed out.

Laughing, Max took another sip from his glass then added, "He's lucky to have you."

"I wouldn't go that far."

"I would." Max wrapped his fingers over the other guy's hand. Slowly, Patrick's attention slid upward from where they were joined. His gaze connected with Max's, and the rest of the world fell away, heightening his senses. The feel of Patrick's skin next to his was electric, frying his ability to think.

And he wanted more. More of the redhead's body against his.

Patrick's mouth parted, revealing the tip of his tongue right before he licked his bottom lip. Max's cock swelled, going rock-hard at the sight. Damn, he couldn't seem to control his dick around Patrick. One look, one glimpse of his tongue, and he had a hard-on. This shit was becoming embarrassing.

"I hope you boys enjoyed your dinner," Pops said, placing

the check on the table.

Tugging his hand free and straightening his shoulders, Patrick replied first. "It was great. Thank you."

"Yes, it was delicious as always," Max added.

"Good, good." Pops beamed. "I'll collect this whenever you're ready," he said, tapping the pocket folder with their bill. "No hurry."

Pops moved away, and the silence between them grew thunderous. Patrick pulled out his wallet, but Max quickly headed him off and stuffed enough bills inside the holder to cover the check plus a generous tip. "I got this," Max said.

"I can pay for my own meal," Patrick added, his jaw tight. "I'm the one who asked you to meet me, remember?"

"I know. But—"

"But, what?" His gaze narrowed. "I might not be in the same position as I was in a couple of years ago, but I don't need a handout."

"I realize that. I was just trying—"

Patrick yanked some cash from his billfold and tossed it onto the table in front of Max. "That should cover my half of the meal, plus drinks." He pushed from the booth.

"Wait." Max gathered the bills. The last thing he'd wanted to do was offend him by picking up the check. *Shit!* How had the evening gone downhill so fast? "Patrick!" He hurried after him, but the redhead was already heading through the door.

Shouldering through the exit after him, Max spotted Patrick rounding the corner at the end of the block. Damn, he could move fast. Max picked up his pace, and within seconds, he made his way around the building.

"Patrick! Hang on."

The other guy stopped beside a faded blue pickup, but didn't turn to face him. Max caught up with him and grasped his wrist. Patrick glanced his way, his expression telegraphing that hanging around any longer was the last thing he wanted to be doing.

"Listen," the former jock began. "I appreciate your help. I really do. But like my father always taught me, a Guinness pays his own way." He sighed. "I don't want or need your money."

"Okay." Max nodded. "Point made." No one had to school him on the fact that Patrick Guinness was all man. And Max hadn't been trying to insinuate otherwise by wanting to cover their bill. Taking two more steps forward, he narrowed the space between them. "Since we're getting things straight here, let me clear something up." Fuck, he smelled good, like sunshine and sandalwood. His pulse spiked, making it hard for him to focus. "I wasn't trying to buy you or flaunt my money. I enjoyed your company and wanted to buy you dinner. That's it."

"Right," Patrick said, yet the hard lines around his mouth showed he wasn't convinced.

Max lifted a brow. "If you want, next time can be on you."

"Next time, huh?" Patrick barked out a brief laugh. "You think me and you should have dinner again?"

Max shrugged. "Why not?"

"Why would you want to?" His expression twisted as if in confusion.

"Because of this." Before Max could give himself another second to think about the consequences, he grabbed Patrick by the front of his shirt and sealed his lips over the other guy's. The redhead's breath hitched at the contact, his body tensing beneath Max's fingers. Max tilted his head, opened his mouth, and deepened the kiss. Patrick responded, his hands cupping the back of Max's head, holding him steady. Someone groaned, but he had no idea at the moment who. All he could think about was how good the guy kissed. He was perfection against Max's mouth, his flesh.

Patrick jerked his head away, his fingertips biting into

Max's scalp. The sharp sting should've hurt. Instead, a sizzling arrow of pleasure shot straight to the head of his cock.

"Dammit," Max moaned. "I want you."

Groaning, Patrick's hands slid from Max's head and pushed him back. "We need to stop."

What? Max shoved his fingers through his hair as if the action could somehow help his brain to make sense of what had just happened. "What's wrong?"

Patrick rounded the front of his truck, shaking his head. "Everything about this—you and me—that's what." Patrick jerked his truck's door open. "I gotta go." He climbed inside and was gone before Max could form a coherent thought.

Shit... He slumped against the parking meter. He'd royally screwed up. Handled the moment all wrong.

He understood they came from different worlds, but did that have to mean they would be a mistake? Max sighed and straightened, heading farther down the block toward his BMW.

His father would certainly agree with Patrick. He would lose his mind if he knew his son, his heir, was dating a man outside of their social circle. Shit. Any man at all if he wanted to go public.

Indulging in a romantic entanglement with someone of whom his father approved would make life so much easier. Although it would mean he'd have to suddenly morph into a heterosexual male. Unfortunately for his father, he couldn't change who he was at his core to soothe his dad's discomfort with his sexuality.

Not going to happen.

He opened the door to this car and lowered himself onto the driver's seat. The ventilated leather sighed under his weight. He closed his eyes, still unable to shake the feel of the other man's lips against his.

"Dammit!" He slammed a fist against the wheel. No one

had ever made him feel so alive. Made him burn. The idea of avoiding each other simply because of the differences in their bank accounts made his dinner revolt. He inhaled deep, forcing the nausea back down.

How can that kind of chemistry between two people be wrong?

Chapter Six

What had he been thinking, allowing his lust to overrule his head? The other night had not been a date. Patrick had met Max for dinner to discuss Liam's situation. So why had it been sheer hell trying to focus? No one got inside his head and made him crazy like Max did. All he'd wanted to think about at Bella's was how damn good Max looked in his crisp teal dress shirt. How the color had made his blue eyes appear even more captivating, especially in contrast to his dark hair. And that damn kiss. *Shit.* The moment Max's lips had touched his, a spark had ignited inside his veins.

"Earth to Pat!" Tommie's voice dragged him back to the present. "You still with me?"

"What?" Patrick blinked and started adding the column of numbers again on his calculator. "Yeah. I'm here. I'm just focused on closing out today's invoices."

"Sure you are." Tommie dragged over a chair, plopped onto the seat and propped his boots on top of Patrick's desk. "You're worried about Liam. Did you meet with that attorney friend of yours?"

"I did." Patrick groaned inside his head. Tommie knew he was bisexual and had no problem with it, but he wasn't about to dish about his and Max's past or the details of how their "meeting" had ended. "We had dinner a couple of nights ago. Max said he'd talk to one of the firm's associates about Liam's case."

"Good." Tommie nodded. "That's good. Any news since then?"

"Not yet," he said, doing his best to hide the stress from his tone. He hoped like hell how he'd gone off on Max after the kiss hadn't changed things. Damn. He'd always had a hot temper. But something inside him said Max wasn't the kind of guy who'd let Liam go down because of a personal issue with his brother. Even on the first night they'd met, it was easy to tell that Max was a decent guy. If it weren't for the fact they came from such different places, he could easily get caught up…

What the hell was I thinking? PG doesn't do relationships.

How was he supposed to fit anyone, male or female, inside his world? He had to keep his head straight. Focus on Liam and the business. Keep the place above water, not just for him and brother, but also for the other guys counting on him for a job. He didn't have time for shit like romance or love.

"But no news is good news, right?" Patrick glanced up at Tommie. "He hasn't called to tell me no one would take Liam's case."

"That's something, I guess."

"You're no damn help, you know that?" He threw an empty can at the other guy. Tommie easily deflected it, sending it bouncing off the office wall and clattering onto the concrete floor. "Aren't you the older and wiser one around here? You're supposed to agree with me. Encourage me."

"Hey! I never claimed to be Dr. Phil." He moved forward in his chair, his boots thumping onto the floor. "My skills are better utilized in other places." He grinned and mock polished his nails against the T-shirt covering his chest. "And trust me, there've been no complaints about my talents from the ladies."

"You are so full of shit." Patrick laughed. "You probably haven't overheard any because you're done so fast and out the door, they don't have time to bitch."

He barked a laugh. "Fuck you!"

"You wish."

"Your ass ain't my type."

"You're not that picky, dude. Any ass is your—" The rest of his sentence was cut off by a knock on the glass of the front door.

"Who the hell is that?" Patrick pushed away from his desk and stood.

"Whoever it is apparently can't read, since the closed sign is in front of their face," Tommie said.

Patrick maneuvered around the counter and into the lobby. Through the glass, he spotted the profile of a man with wavy dark hair, a white dress shirt, and dark navy slacks. His midsection tightened. Excitement at seeing Max thrummed through his chest. He sucked in a stabilizing breath. Maybe he hadn't fucked everything up?

Pulling the shop's keys from his pocket, Patrick strode toward the door and slid the proper one into the deadbolt. With a slight twist of his wrist, the lock released a metallic *click*, and he shoved the door open. Max pivoted, facing him at the sound.

"Hey," he said. "I'm sorry to show up after hours unannounced like this, but I thought I'd take the chance that you'd still be here. I wanted to deliver the news in person."

"No problem." Patrick stood back, allowing him to come in. "I still have some paperwork to do, so your timing was good." With Patrick leading the way, Max followed him behind the counter. "Max, you remember Tommie from the other day, right?"

"Yes, I do." Max stretched out his hand. Tommie stood and accepted his palm, giving it a shake. "Nice to see you again."

"Likewise." Tommie turned and headed toward the shop area. "I'm going to get of here and leave you two to talk." At the door, he glanced over his shoulder at Max. "I hope you have the news for Pat he's hoping to hear. Liam is a good kid. He's just dealing with some stuff the only way he knows how right now."

"I understand," Max said. "I'm going to do everything I can to help."

"I'm glad to hear that." Tommie nodded then made his exit.

"Tommie's like family," Patrick said. "He's been working here since he was around twenty. My dad gave him a chance when no one else would, and he's been loyal ever since." *Shit.* He couldn't turn his mouth off. He was acting like a kid in the presence of his childhood crush, talking about everything but the elephant in the room. The kiss. The sexual tension between them that could ignite a stick of dynamite. But there was no need to talk about it, because he and Max weren't going to happen again.

Patrick returned to the seat at his desk, and Max took Tommie's chair across from him. "Why wouldn't anyone else hire him?"

"Let's just say he got into some trouble as a kid and the situation made finding a job a problem."

"Sounds like your dad had good instincts about people."

"Most of the time." God how he missed him. Missed his advice. His wisdom. "He was the best. And so is Tommie." He placed his forearms on his desk, closing some of the distance between them. "I know he'd always have me and Liam's back."

"You can't put a price on having a friend like that," Max said.

"That's for sure." Patrick snagged a pen from his desk, mindlessly working it between his fingers. Max needed to get to the point before he jumped out of his skin. Or jumped on something, or someone, he'd later regret. "Anyway, you said you were here with some news."

"Yes." Pulling his chair closer, Max folded his arms onto the other side of Patrick's desk. "I spoke with one of the firm's partners, Tom Gibson, and he's agreed to take Liam's case. He's an excellent attorney. Liam will be in good hands."

Closing his eyes, Patrick drew in a breath of relief. "That's the best news I've heard all day." He still had no idea how he'd pay for it, but he'd find a way. He'd do anything for his brother.

Max smiled. "I'm glad I could be the one to deliver it." He reached into his pocket and pulled out a card. "Call this number on Monday, and Abbie will help set up a time to meet with Tom."

Patrick took the card and stuffed it in his shirt's pocket. "I can't tell you how relieved I am to know Liam is going to have decent representation."

Max went on to explain that since Liam is a first-time offender, the judge might grant him a conditional discharge with community service and an opportunity to have his record expunged if he kept his nose clean. "But Tom will take the time to explain all of this in detail."

"Man, I tell you..." Patrick shook his head. "That sounds really good." He looked at Max, and for a moment he was spellbound, unable to remember a damn good reason why he didn't have the guy bent over his desk. His cock slammed balls deep, Max begging to come as Patrick plowed in and out of his tight ass. His dick hardened at the image, his zipper imprinting itself on the backside of his shaft.

Fuck!

He shook his head as if there were a chance in hell he could erase the fantasy from his brain.

"So how is your brother doing?" Max asked, pulling Patrick back from his thoughts.

"Okay, I guess." Patrick sighed. "Not that I would know. He's had little to say to me since I bailed him out. But he finishes class this week. At least he'll have done something positive over his break. He's been taking a summer course, trying to bring his math grade up so he can graduate with his class next year and hopefully land a football scholarship."

"Give him some time," Max said, his smile gentle, soothing. "He's probably still freaked out about having been arrested." Reaching over, he laid his palm over the back of Patrick's hand, stealing his reason. Just like that—with one touch the guy held the power to shut down his ability to think. "He knows you have his back."

"I hope so," Patrick muttered, the rest of his body frozen by the clasp of one man's fingers on his. He should pull away. Get the hell up from his chair and go home. Leave right now. Not screw up Liam's best chance at getting out of this mess. Besides, Max couldn't possibly want more than a dirty trip across the wrong side of the tracks, a reminder of the one wild night they shared.

Sure, for the last couple of years, hookups at Proclivity had been all Patrick needed. The sex—the physical release— was enough.

But Max wasn't some anonymous ass. They shared a history, albeit a brief one. A night that he'd never gotten out of his system, no matter how many Johns or Janes he fucked. None of them had ever left him marked. It was the only word that fit, that described how he'd felt when he'd left Max's bed that morning after their night together.

The men and women who came to play at the club didn't care who he was, and vice versa. He didn't care who they were, either, or what they thought. However, when it came to Max... What Max thought of him, and the reason the guy wanted to be with him...mattered.

Mentally, he rolled his eyes.

Christ, he was pathetic.

A beep sounded from his cell, jarring him back into the moment. Patrick pulled his hand away and checked the display on his smartphone. "Speaking of my brother," he said. "He's wondering where the hell I am." Patrick glanced over at Max. "The kid's always hungry, and I promised I'd bring home dinner."

"Oh, right." Max stood. "It's getting late, and I should be getting home, too. I still have some work to do."

"What?" Patrick pulled his keys from his pocket. "It's Friday night."

"I can't afford to not be prepared for the bar," Max said, following him to the door. "It's going to be here whether I'm ready or not."

Patrick unlocked the door and held it open for Max. He brushed past, and the familiar scent that was uniquely Max filled his nostril. How the dude managed to smell like a summer day and an ocean breeze was crazy. He breathed deep, soaking it in. Addictive.

"You'll be ready," Patrick managed to utter. "You got this, Blue Eyes. You were meant for this."

Max looked back, sporting a grin that showed off his perfect white teeth. Damn. He was almost too beautiful to be a guy.

"What's that smile all about?" Patrick leaned against the doorjamb, shoving his hands into his jeans pockets.

"You called me 'Blue Eyes,'" Max said. "I haven't heard that nickname since...you know."

"Oh…" *Shit.* He hadn't even realized he'd—

"It's okay," Max said, interrupting his momentary panic. "I don't mind when you call me that. And don't worry." He shook his head, backtracking toward his car. "I know it doesn't mean anything. I'm sure it was reflex."

"Reflex." Patrick nodded. "I guess that's what it was." At least that was as good an explanation as any. He wasn't about to dive any deeper into his psyche about that slip. He didn't want to think about how much he wished Max wasn't getting into his car. How much he wished he were staying a little longer, exploring just how bad or good it would be if he gave in, allowed himself to savor one more taste of his…

Fuck. Bad idea, Guinness.

But damn if he couldn't help it. Couldn't help wondering how bad could bad be.

Forty-five minutes later, Patrick slapped his keys on the kitchen island along with a couple of bags of takeout.

"Finally!" Liam said, coming from the hallway and into the kitchen. "I was about five minutes from calling the FBI for Mulder and Scully. I figured you'd been kidnapped on the way home by aliens or something."

"Ha ha," Patrick said, and grabbed one of the bags, tossing it at Liam. "Food. Eat. Since I'm sure your stomach was what you were worried about and not my well-being. You were scared the aliens were going to eat your BBQ."

His brother snagged the package in mid-air, then rummaged inside, pulling his sandwich free. "Truth." Liam shrugged. "You know me so well."

"I love you, too, jackass."

Liam snickered.

"By the way, I have some news on the attorney front," Patrick said, hauling his dinner over to the table. He dropped into a chair at the end.

"Oh yeah?" Liam bit off a mouthful of his sandwich on

the way to the fridge and returned with two bottles of Coke in one hand. "So what did you find out?"

"Tom Gibson at Segreti Law Firm has agreed to take your case." Patrick twisted the cap on his soda and the plastic gave way, releasing a pop under his grip.

"Segreti?" Liam settled onto a chair and lowered his sandwich onto the scarred oak. "Wasn't that your ex's last name? Please tell me you didn't call Max about me."

"It's not exactly like we have a legal team at our beck and call, Liam," Patrick said. "Max was our best connection for a decent attorney to help you out of this shit."

"I can't believe you spilled everything about me to Mr. Hot Pants Moneybags," he said. "What did you promise him in return if he agreed to help me?"

The jab hit Patrick directly in the chest, the point needle-sharp, driving all the way home where it hurt. "Is that really what you think of me? That I'd just whore myself out to some guy to get what I want?"

"No, I-I…" Liam deflected his gaze, picking at his sandwich. "That wasn't what I meant." He looked up. "You said it yourself—what do you two have in common? I was surprised you'd called him, that's all." His brother took a gulp of his Coke. "And now Mr. Moneybags knows all about my arrest, the marijuana." He glared at Patrick. "That I'm such a problem for you."

"That's not what he's going to think—and it's not how I feel!" He'd hoped the news about finding an attorney would brighten their evening. Instead, he may have made things worse between him and his brother. He hadn't meant to embarrass Liam by going to Max. Christ. He had no idea Liam would feel ashamed or betrayed. If he had, no way in hell would he have done it.

"Sure." Liam snatched his sandwich, shoved it into the bag, and grabbed his drink. "Whatever." His chair scrapped against the wood as he stood and hauled ass from the room. A moment later, the door to his room slammed shut.

"Fine!" Patrick yelled out. "Don't talk to me." Frustration burned a heated path into his face. How had Dad stayed sane with two hardheaded boys? "Stay in your damn room," he added. "It's safer that way."

What the fuck was he supposed to do now?

Chapter Seven

"Come on, Max," Abbie groaned. "Live a little."

"Wow," Max said. "I'm experiencing a serious case of déjà vu right now." He took a swallow of his sweet iced tea. "You said almost the exact same thing to me on another Saturday night not too many years ago, when you and a bunch of your friends went on a pub crawl. And if I remember correctly, you ended up sick for two days straight."

"Point taken." She swirled the tiny straw inside the tumbler containing her margarita on the rocks. "But this is Bernie's! They have some of the best drinks in town. You could have at least ordered a Long Island Iced Tea, for God's sake." She sipped from her glass. "It's the weekend, my friend. You deserve to relax."

"You know I don't like to drink when I'm studying for an exam. I'll relax after I finish sitting for the bar next week."

Before she could respond, a tall guy, his blond hair trimmed close to the scalp, rounded their table. "Hey, Abbie," the stranger said, his hand brushing her shoulder.

Max couldn't help but admire Abbie's new friend. He

looked good in his well-worn jeans, rips in all the right places, and a black T-shirt tucked in at his waist. The material hugged his torso and showcased his build. *You go, girl.*

The guy was very nice looking, but he didn't hold a candle to someone else he knew. Someone whose ripped body had held a permanent starring role in every one of his fantasies for the last three years.

"Max, this is Damian Hill," Abbie said. Damian slid onto the seat at the table next to him. "Damian, this is Max Segreti." The blond stuck out his hand and Max slid his palm into his for a shake. The other guy's gaze raked Max from top to bottom with a hungry look that had nothing to do with food. Max glanced over at Abbie, who sat there with a self-satisfied smile. Oh, hell… What had she done?

"As I mentioned before, Damian, Max is a law graduate and works at the firm with me," Abbie said.

Mentioned before?

How long had she been planning this ambush? He was starting to feel like a piece of meat up for sale.

"Well, it is his dad's firm, but Max isn't exactly getting any special treatment," she went on to say. "He's working his ass off."

Over his glass, Max sent Abbie a "don't try to kiss up to me now" glare. *You know you ambushed me, and you knew I would be pissed as hell.*

Ignoring his look, Abbie added, "Max, Damien is a personal trainer at my gym. He's so impressive to watch in action, everyone wants a session with him."

"Thanks," Damian said. "That's kind of you to say, but all the trainers there are great."

"Don't be so modest," she said. "He's being modest, Max." She tipped up her tumbler, downing the last of her margarita, then surveyed the room in an exaggerated fashion. "Where's our server?" She groaned. "I'm going to get us another round."

Abbie stood and started to stroll away, but Max grabbed her arm. He curled a finger, beckoning her closer. She tucked her hair behind her ear and bent over.

"Payback is hell," he whispered.

She laughed. Actually *laughed* at his misery. Then she slapped his arm and slipped away. At that moment, a guy entering the pub caught his eye. *Patrick.* The name sighed inside his head, and his pulse skipped a beat.

He couldn't help but follow Patrick's progress as he made his way to a seat at the bar.

"So, what's it like working with your father?" Damian's question sliced through the noise of the crowd.

"What's that?" Max tugged his attention back to the guy at the table. Damian moved his chair closer and snaked his arm around Max's back before repeating himself. His breath warmed the shell of Max's ear, and his stomach roiled. Damn, his automatic response to the man's question wasn't an invitation for a make-out session.

"It's not so bad," Max replied, pulling away and trying to reclaim some distance. His gaze flicked back toward Patrick at the bar. The former player sat with a beer in hand, but he wasn't facing the array of liquor bottles or the flat screen mounted above them. Patrick's attention was fixed on Max and the blond sitting beside him. But his expression was a stoic mask.

Shit.

The guy was damn good at hiding his emotions. Max had no idea if seeing him with another man was pissing Patrick off or if he didn't give a flying fuck. But the fact that Patrick hadn't stopped staring at the two of them said he wasn't totally unaffected. That was something, at least. Maybe there was a sliver of interest.

"I have another drink coming, so our server should be here in a minute," Abbie said, dropping back into her seat.

"Great." Damian smiled. "I could use a beer."

As if he had conjured their server, she appeared at the table with Abbie's drink in hand.

"What are you drinking, Max?" Damian nodded at his nearly empty tumbler. "I got this round."

"It's just sweet tea. But I'm good. Really." Max smoothed his palms over the denim surrounding his thighs, ready to bolt. Between Damian's unwanted attention and Patrick being seated mere feet away, yet totally out of reach, he was about to come unglued. "I need to be leaving soon, anyway."

"What?" The bottom of Abbie's glass thumped onto the tabletop. "We just got here."

"I know, but I can't relax knowing I should be preparing for the bar exam," he said.

"One drink," Damian added, wrapping his fingers around Max's wrist and tugging his hand a little closer. Christ. It was all he could do not to rip his arm away. But he didn't want to hurt Abbie's feelings. The blond smiled. "We've barely gotten a chance to talk."

With a deep inhale, Max gently retrieved his hand, stalling the reflex to jerk it back. "I know," he said. "I'm sorry about that, but I really hadn't planned to be out late tonight." Max stood. "It was great to meet you, though."

"Max," Abbie moaned. "I wish you'd hang out a little longer."

"Next time, okay?" He placed a peck on her cheek followed by a look that said they *would* talk later.

Before heading straight for the exit, Max made a detour for the men's room. His head was a mess, and he needed a few minutes to regroup before going home and cracking the books again. Inside, he used the facilities then went to the sink to wash his hands.

He couldn't believe Abbie had arranged a blind date behind his back. God, he hated being set up, and she knew that. And what were the odds that Patrick, of all people, would show up at the same time and place, making things even more awkward. He shook his head. Behind him, the door opened. *Shit!* He'd been so preoccupied he'd forgotten to press the lock. Good thing whoever it was hadn't walked in a minute earlier.

"Sorry," Max called out. "I'm heading out, so it's all yours." He glanced up at the mirror and the air stalled in his lungs when he saw the man's reflection in the background. "Patrick," he breathed.

Grabbing a handful of paper towels from the machine next to him, he pivoted and faced him, clearing his suddenly dry throat. "I was just leaving."

He started for the door, but Patrick twisted and locked it. As if he'd just hit a double shot of espresso, Max's pulse spiked.

"What are you doing?" Max tossed the damp towels into the bin.

Like a sentinel guarding a drawbridge, Patrick leaned his back against the door and crossed his arms. "So, how long have you been seeing him?"

"By 'him,' I assume you mean Damian?" *What the hell? Is he jealous?*

"How would I know his name?" Patrick scowled. "I'm just wondering how long you've been seeing him."

Matching his stance, Max crossed him arms. "That's not what you're wondering at all," he said.

"So you're a mind reader now, as well as an attorney?" Patrick marched away from the door, eating up the space between them until Max's back was pressed against the opposite wall of the narrow bathroom. But Max wasn't afraid. He knew Patrick's aggressive move had nothing to do with anger. He'd seen the exact same storm brewing in his eyes before, and he remembered it all too well. The look wasn't violence or rage. It was passion and dominance.

And it was exciting as hell.

Patrick slapped his palms against the tile on either side of Max's head, boxing him in. "If you know my mind so damn well, why don't you tell me what I was wondering."

"You wanted to know if Damian has fucked me." The words tumbled from his lips like a raging river that had crested a waterfall, its momentum so great that there was no way to keep it from going over.

Unable to look away from the rapid rise and fall of the other man's chest, he curled his fingers in tight at his sides. It took every ounce of his control not to run his hands under the hem of Patrick's shirt and smooth his palms over the ridges of the man's washboard abs. Then he'd slide lower. *Oh, hell yeah.* He was dying to hear the redhead's moan again as he stroked the thick cock he knew hid behind his jeans.

A low rumble reverberated in the other man's chest, drawing Max's attention upward. Patrick's eyes were narrowed, his stare heated, and Max could have sworn it burned right through to his soul. His voice rusty, his former lover asked, "Did he?"

A part of Max wanted to clam up, leave him to wonder. What the hell did it matter who he fucked or who fucked him? He and Patrick had been a one-time deal, and according to him, they were never going to happen again. But the next thing Max knew, the truth was falling off his tongue.

"No," Max whispered.

Air rushed from Patrick's lungs as if he'd been holding his breath in anticipation of Max's answer. One sinful corner of his mouth lifted, right before the coarse hairs of his five o'clock shadow brushed Max's cheek. The warmth of his breath heated his neck. "You want *me* to fuck you, Max?"

A hard shiver raced down Max's spine, and his eyelids shuttered. *Oh, hell. So damn bad.* His cock throbbed.

"Is that what you want?" Patrick pulled his head away.

Max opened his eyes at the same moment Patrick's palm brushed the swollen ridge of his cock, scorching whatever part of his brain was responsible for language. Max groaned.

"I'll take that as a yes." Patrick yanked on Max's belt, quickly loosening its hold.

"Patrick," Max gasped. "We can't—"

"Can't what?" The redhead already had the button and fly open on Max's jeans. He reached inside, wrapping his fingers around Max's stiff shaft.

"Shit," Max grunted, and latched onto Patrick's solid torso for support.

"You like my fist around your cock, don't you?" Patrick pulled Max free, stroking his length. *Fuck, yes.* Max's eyes rolled back under the onslaught of pleasure.

"That's not the point," he managed to get out. Patrick's tempo increased, and Max couldn't stop the shudder rocking his body. He closed his eyes, lost in sensation. *Stop.* He really should tell him to stop. He had to keep his head on straight. "We can't…we can't fuck here," he finally managed to mutter.

The firm stroke of Patrick's hand vanished, and Max choked back a curse at the loss. But hadn't he been the one to call it? God, he could be such a stupid idiot.

"Who said we were going to fuck?"

Startled at the other man's response, Max opened his eyes to find Patrick unzipping his jeans. The redhead's thick cock sprang free, the broad head glistening with pre-cum under the florescent light.

"We're not?" Max rasped, his voice nearly lost from the delicious sight. His palm itched to stroke the heavily veined length of his lover's shaft. The memory of the way his cock had stretched and burned him pushing deep inside, pleasure and pain blurring, was still so damn vivid. "But…"

"I'm giving us a taste. The quick release we both seem to

need so damn bad." Pressing his hips in closer, he fisted Max's erection once more. "Wrap your hand around my cock. Press me against the backside of yours." Max did as instructed, locking their shafts together. Patrick rocked against him, air hissing from between his teeth. Max groaned at the exquisite feel of the other man's cock sliding over his sensitized flesh.

Up and down they stroked one another, rocking in time with hungry, needy jerks.

"Faster," Patrick demanded. "Fuck." His free hand found its way into the hair at back of Max's head. His fingertips curled into the strands, the blunt tips scraping against Max's scalp. But it wasn't painful. Just the opposite. The sting heated his blood even more, had his balls drawing tighter, had him teetering on the edge of climax.

"Damn...Patrick." Max panted. "Almost there." He glanced down at the point where their bodies were joined. The sight of their cocks, sticky with pre-cum, sliding, surging against each other, greedy for the next stroke of pleasure, was his tipping point. "Oh, fuck," he grunted. "I'm coming."

"Do it," Patrick ordered, his voice gritty and raw. "Come for me, baby."

Max's orgasm roared up his shaft, the storm violent, yet exhilarating at the same time. The sensation stole his next breath. But he didn't really care. Oxygen could come later. All he needed was the next wave. The next stroke of Patrick's hand. The next touch of the other man's flesh against his.

"Fuck, yes." Patrick moaned. "That's it." His lips brushed against Max's, the effect triggering Max's diaphragm, and he gasped. A tremor rocked Patrick's body, and he grunted. "You're making me come so hard." A hot rush of liquid coated Max's already drenched fingers. Patrick's mouth sealed over Max's, and the other male groaned into the kiss. Max opened, inviting him in. Patrick slipped inside, rhythmically shuttling his tongue along his, as if he could somehow sense every pump of Max's orgasm up his cock.

Damn it all to hell. He would give anything, sell his soul to the devil himself, if he could freeze time at that moment.

But like all good things, it ended too soon. Patrick pulled back, breaking the spell. "We should get cleaned up and out of here before someone knocks on the door," his lover said, his tone shifting from seduction to business without missing a beat.

"Yeah, you're right," Max said, but Patrick was already at the sink, washing his hands.

"I'll go first," Patrick said, yanking a few paper towels from the dispenser. "Wait a couple of minutes, then you leave."

"Got it." Max took his turn at the sink.

"Okay." Patrick finished zipping up and turned for the door.

"Wait a minute, dammit." He wasn't about to walk out without another word, as if nothing had happened between them. It wasn't like Max expected them to get engaged, but he expected more than a brush off.

Patrick drew to a halt, but he didn't look back.

"Is that how you're going to leave it?" Max twisted the faucet, shutting off the water, and faced the other man's back. "You come in here all hot and bothered, we jack each other off, and then you walk out without so much as a 'see ya later,' or 'thanks for the service'?"

Patrick's fist tightened around the doorknob. "Wasn't this what you wanted from me?" He glanced over his shoulder. "A quick hookup for old time's sake?"

"I never said that's all you were to me, and you know that!" Max slammed the wad of paper towels in his hand into the trash.

"Please…" Patrick rolled his eyes. "Like you would ever want anything more than sex with someone like me—a grease monkey."

He didn't give a damn that Patrick worked in an auto shop. But was he ready to take things to the next level, knowing the kind of resistance and struggle they'd both be facing from his father? The denial was right there on his tongue, but it sat there a minute too long. And Patrick knew it. Max's hesitation was all the validation he'd needed.

"Yeah." Patrick nodded. "That's what I thought." He twisted the doorknob, popping the lock, and walked out of the bathroom.

Out of Max's life.

The door swung closed behind his lover with a loud *clank*, and the hollow sound pinged off the tile walls and into the empty pit Max had once called his stomach.

Placing his palm over his center, Max massaged his midsection. *This has to be what people call "feeling gutted."*

He'd spent most of his life by himself, alone in his room studying. Yet the isolation had never bothered him. Max surveyed the space around him—the tiny space he no longer shared with Patrick. His chest tightened, squeezing the air from his lungs. *Fuck...* Sinking onto his haunches, he captured his head in his hands, digging his fingers into his scalp. How could he already miss Patrick so damn much?

Chapter Eight

Patrick stared at the elegant black font scrolling *Segreti Law Firm* across the glass double doors.

Segreti.

The name pinged off the walls of his skull. For too many days, he hadn't been able to get one certain Segreti off his mind. He flashed back to the vision of Max against the wall, his blue eyes glassy with euphoria as his cock erupted, spilling hot and wet over his knuckles. Patrick sucked in a stabilizing breath, willing the image aside. He couldn't think about that now. Not here.

Reflex had him flexing the fingers of one hand at his side for control as he pulled open the door with his other. Liam went in ahead of him, his shoulders slumped beneath his graphic T-shirt. Anyone watching would have sworn Patrick was marching the boy off to the guillotine and not to meet the attorney who would hopefully help keep his ass out of jail.

If either of them should have reason to hesitate breeching the door of the firm, it was the elder brother. Having to see Max again after the way he'd left things several days ago wasn't Patrick's idea of fun. The guy had done them a solid speaking to Mr. Gibson on Liam's behalf, and he felt like a real ass having hooked up with Max—in a bathroom of all places. Mentally, he grimaced.

Max deserved better than that.

Deserved someone better than a guy who'd jack him off against a wall and walk out after the fact. But he'd totally lost it when he'd spotted Max with some other guy. Then when the blond had reached over and put his hands on him… Patrick cringed at the memory. There had been no way he could have left that pub without finding what else the asshole had had his hands on.

So when Max had left the table for the bathroom, he couldn't resist the chance to get him alone to find out. But he hadn't intended on things going as far as they had.

Yep, you're a real class act, Guinness.

Locking them in that room together had been a mistake. The heat between them had been too much. The close proximity had only fanned the flames, driving him even crazier. He'd had to find a way quench the fire. Except that touching the attorney again…he may as well have poured gasoline on the simmering, incessant need for the guy that he'd been trying to suppress.

They'd both left burned.

Hell, maybe there was a part of him that had wanted to punish Max because of his own loss of control.

He couldn't imagine Max ever wanting to see him again. And he wouldn't blame him. He didn't deserve the things Patrick had said. Even if the part about Max not wanting anything more because of their class differences was true, something inside told him Max wasn't a player.

"Damn…" His brother's curse jerked Patrick back into the present. "Get a load of this place."

Patrick scanned the cavernous lobby, from the vaulted

ceiling with its enormous chandelier to the marble-inlaid columns that graced both ends of the rooms. Paintings that screamed wealth hung on the walls, depicting serene nature themes from waterfalls to mountaintops. Patrick checked the buttons down the front of his shirt and rotated his shoulders. He couldn't remember the last time he'd been more uncomfortable.

"Seriously, Pat," his brother said, snagging his arm and pulling him to the side before they reached the front desk. "How the hell are we supposed to pay for a dude like this to handle my case?"

"Don't worry about it," Patrick said and grasped his brother's shoulder. "I got it covered." He tugged at Liam, hoping he'd drop the subject and do as he was told.

"What does that mean?" Liam bit out, his expression grim.

"Liam…" Patrick rumbled. "For once, would you just do what I say and let me handle this?"

Liam crossed his arms. "No way in hell am I going in there until you tell me what you've done."

Shit! The punk could be so damn hardheaded. And if Patrick were being straight with himself, he'd admit Liam reminded him too much of himself at that age. Thank God he'd grown out of some of that defiance.

Yeah, right.

"Fine." Patrick sighed, closing his eyes and silently praying for strength to deal with the backlash from his brother. Opening his eyes, Patrick gripped his brother's upper arm. "Let's do this outside."

"Whatever," Liam groaned and headed for the door.

They both exited the office, and Patrick moved them away from the glass doors before facing Liam once more. "Before we talk, I need you to promise me you won't blow up and take off. That you'll keep your cool." With his mouth drawn into a hard line, Liam glared back at him. "I need you to keep it together and follow through with meeting this attorney, Liam." Patrick braced his hands on his hips.

"I ain't promising a damn thing until I hear what you've got to say."

"Dammit, bro." Patrick shook his head. "Sometimes talking to you is like beating my skull against a wall."

"Well, you never listen," Liam spat back.

"I never—" Christ, his head was going to explode. "Oh my God." Patrick scrubbed a palm over his face.

"For fuck's sake, just tell me what you've done already." Liam crossed his arms.

Digging deep for every ounce of patience he could find, Patrick looked down at his brother. "Like you said, we need money for a good attorney. So I did what I had to. I went to the bank and borrowed some money against the business."

"You did what?" Liam's expression morphed from quiet disdain to disgust. "That's all we have. You can't risk the business for me!" Liam slammed his palms into Patrick's chest, shoving him back, but Patrick quickly recovered his balance.

"I'm not going to allow you to destroy your future because of one screw up!" he yelled at his brother.

Liam paced back and forth, a low groan rolling off him. "I can't believe you did that." He shook his head. "What if business falls off and you can't pay it back?" Liam stopped in front of him. "Did you think of that? What will you do then?"

"Of course I thought about that. It's not going to happen." Shit. The look of panic on his brother's face was killing him. "I promise you. It's not going to happen. Things have been good."

"You don't know that." Liam's head fell forward, his chest heaving. "What if it doesn't and you have to close the doors? It's not just us who'll be fucked, but Tommie, too." Liam looked up, his eyes welling with unshed tears. "All because of me, Pat."

At that moment, Patrick would have given anything to take away his brother's fears, his pain. To give him a one hundred percent guarantee that nothing was going to go wrong. Wrapping his hands around Liam's upper arms, he pulled him close, forcing him to meet his gaze. "I promise you, I'm going to do everything in my power to make sure that doesn't happen. But you are my first priority. You're my brother, my blood. And I refuse to allow this mistake to haunt you. So we're going to walk back in there and see what this guy can do to fix this situation. You know why?"

"Why?" Liam grunted.

"Because you're worth it." Placing a palm to the back of his brother's neck, Patrick yanked him in for a hug. Liam tensed under his hold, but after a moment, his brother's arms were around him, squeezing him in return. Patrick's heart swelled, and moisture clouded his vision. Maybe something good had come out of this nightmare.

"All right. All right." Liam extracted himself from Patrick's hold, shrugging his shoulders as if he were contaminated. "Jesus. Enough with the touchy-feely shit."

"I'm done." Patrick held up his hands in surrender. "That's all you're getting out of me."

"Thank God. Let's get this over with." Liam marched toward the door.

Patrick rolled his eyes and followed after him. So this is what it felt like to actually win a round with his brother. A smile tugged the corners of his mouth.

Inside, Patrick approached the front desk and informed the receptionist of his brother Liam's arrival. An attractive woman with long, reddish-brown hair, who appeared to be in her mid-twenties, briefly checked her computer screen then glanced back up at him. "Mr. Gibson will be with you shortly.

Please make yourself comfortable."

"Thanks." Patrick said, but he couldn't keep his gaze from straying to the desks behind the receptionist and searching for a certain dark-haired nerd. Was that where Max spent his day? "Excuse me," he said, drawing her attention once more. *What the hell am I doing?* He groaned internally. But he couldn't stop himself. He had to know. "Is Max Segreti here today?"

She grinned. "Oh, you know Max?"

"Yeah." Patrick nodded, his pulse racing. Damn, his big mouth. "We met back at USC before he went to law school."

"Really," she said, but her smile faltered as if she were trying to piece a puzzle together inside her mind. "Max and I have been friends since then, too. But he's not here today. This is the week he sits for the bar."

"Oh." Patrick's stomach plummeted. But he wasn't sure if it was from disappointment or relief. He shoved his hands in his pockets and turned toward the lobby.

"If I could have your first name," she added, "I'd be happy to tell Max you asked about him."

He glanced over his shoulder at her, and her smile brightened.

Something inside him said he bet she would. Not that she was devious, but he had a hunch she would be more than excited to tell Max that a man had asked about him at the office.

"That's okay." He shook his head. "I'll text him later."

"Okay. If you're sure."

"I'm sure," he said and eased into a vacant chair next to Liam.

Liam nudged his shoulder. "Really? You had to ask for him?"

"It would have been rude to come in here and not say hi," Patrick said. "I was just being polite."

"You're just being hot for him," Liam mumbled.

"Shut it," Patrick muttered under his breath.

"You and Mr. Moneybags have disaster written all over you." Liam kicked back in his seat, crossing his long legs at his ankles. "Can you say, Titanic? Cause that's how badly you're going down."

"My brother, the dark prophet." Patrick rubbed his fingers over his mouth and jaw, shrugging off Liam's warning of doom. But they were only words. Harmless. Nothing would happen if he kept his distance from Max. But that was the problem, wasn't it?

Staying away.

The harder he tried to leave Max alone, the more he wanted to see him. To touch him. Patrick stood, strode toward the wall of windows, and stared out at the manicured view. Liam's predication was more spot-on than his brother knew. Whether he was willing to accept it or not, he was barreling straight for the iceberg known as Max. And the guy was probably going to rip him in two.

Chapter Nine

"So when were you planning to spill about the hunk who came in earlier this week with his brother to see Mr. Gibson?"

Max convulsively swallowed, sending the mouthful of hot coffee down his throat before he was ready, nearly burning out his vocal chords. He coughed. Wheezing, he said, "What?"

"Uh-huh," Abbie said. "Don't play all innocent with me, pretty boy." She laughed. "You know who I'm talking about. Tall—like at least six-foot-four tall—muscular, with auburn hair and green eyes. And if I'm not mistaken, since his brother is Liam, he's none other than Patrick Guinness." Placing one hand on Max's shoulder, Abbie swiveled him around in his chair to face her. "As in *the* Patrick Guinness. Former USC Gamecock's running back drafted to the Packers."

"Patrick Guinness was here?" He shrugged, even though the coffee inside his stomach was about ready to make a return visit. "Wow."

"Come on, Max." She pouted. "How do you know him? You never mentioned him before."

"Who said I know him?" *Play it cool.* "Why would you

think I'd ever met him?"

"Because he asked me if you were working." She grinned. "And he said he knew you from your USC days."

"Oh. He did?" *Damn.* Max twisted his chair back around. His head spun with a list of scenarios as to why Patrick would have brought his name up. He placed his cup on the desk, doing his best to ignore the rapid and heavy thud of his heart.

"Oh?" Abbie came around beside him. "That's all I get? An *oh*?"

"I don't want to talk about it, Abs." And that was the absolute truth. Especially not after the way things had been left between them at the pub. The few heated moments they'd shared in that restroom had been more intense—more alive—than he'd felt with anyone over the last three years. But whatever he'd hoped had begun there that night had been destroyed in the last two minutes, before Patrick had walked out the door.

"Oh my God," she said, her voice hushed. "You two were together back then."

"Abs…" Max groaned and risked a glance up in her direction.

"How did you manage to keep that from me?" She gasped.

"Because we weren't *together* back then," he said.

"But you two did…" Her eyebrows waggled.

He squeezed his eyes shut. There was no going back now. Abbie would never let this go until she pulled it out of him. He opened his eyes. "Once."

"Damn," she drawled. "You and Patrick Guinness." She chewed on her thumbnail, her gaze drifting. "God, I bet he's an animal in the sack."

A beast would be a better word. Except he's the kind of predator where you would give anything to be his prey, to have him take you down.

As if it had been only moments ago and not days, the sensation of the other man's calloused fist wrapping around his cock, stroking him, assaulted his senses. His pulse spiked, sending every ounce of his blood straight to his groin. *Fuck!* He needed a distraction.

"I've got a lot of work to do," Max stated, mentally shaking himself. He flipped open one of the many files stacked on his desk. If only the words didn't resemble some fucking foreign language, he might have some hope of getting the guy out of his thoughts. "This research isn't going to take care of itself."

"In other words, leave it alone, Abbie." She sighed. "You can't blame me for being curious. Dang, Max. It's Patrick Guinness." She straightened. "I can see why you kept it to yourself. Kudos to you on that. I don't know if I could have, if he and I had…you know." She giggled. "One last question, though, please."

"Abbie…" He cocked his head at her.

"Have you two seen each other since you came home? Is that why he asked if you were here?"

At this point, what was the use denying it? "Yes. And yes."

"No wonder you skipped out on me and Damian last weekend." She punched his arm. "If you had told me you were seeing someone…" Abbie shook her head.

"It's not like that between us," he began. "In fact, I'm pretty sure there *isn't* an us."

"Well, I might rethink that if I were you." She smiled. "When I told Patrick you weren't here the other morning, the look on his face said he was disappointed."

"I think you were imagining things." He wasn't about to get his hopes up based on Abbie's assessment of the situation. She was a hopeless romantic.

"Nope. I don't think so." She shook her head. "I know what I saw. Why do you think I couldn't wait to get in here today and ask you about him?" She laughed. "Having yesterday off was torture."

Max couldn't help but chuckle. "You could have called me."

"And miss witnessing the expression on your face when I brought him up? No way! I had to do this in person."

"You're terrible, you know that?" But he didn't know what he'd do without her in his life. She was the bright spot he could always count on.

"I know." She headed back toward her station. "But you love me anyway."

"Which is why I question my sanity on a daily basis," he said.

"Max." Maximo Segreti Sr.'s deep voice cut through the air, giving Max a half-second warning before he rounded the corner. Wearing a perfectly tailored pinstripe suit, his father looked every bit the formidable attorney one didn't dare challenge in court, or in his home. His hairline had begun to recede, but it was still easy to tell Max had inherited his father's dark waves. Most would say he looked more like his father than mother. But whereas the elder Segreti possessed amber-colored eyes, Max had his mother's eyes.

"Good morning, Father," Max said. "What can I help you with?"

"I want to see you in my office." Not waiting for a response, his father turned and left. But that was business as usual. When Maximo Sr. gave a request, no one questioned him.

And that went for Max as well. He followed him down the hall to his large corner office. His father settled behind his oversize glass desk, his outline framed by a wall of windows. "Close the door, please," his father said, leaning back into his plush executive chair.

Max pushed the heavy glass door closed and took one of the seats in front of his father.

"What did you need to see me about?" Max adjusted his tie, the knot suddenly feeling closer to a noose.

"You sat for the bar earlier this week." It was a statement, not a question, since his father was well aware of when he'd sat for the bar. But Max wasn't surprised that he'd waited to speak to him about it at work. There wouldn't be any personal call at home from his father to ask him about how he felt he'd done. Nope. The man was all business.

"That's right."

His father leaned forward, resting his forearms on the glass. "Were you sufficiently prepared?"

"Of course I was prepared." Is that what this was all about? Was he worried that his money had gone to waste, that Max might fail? "When have you ever known me not to be prepared for any exam? I've worked my ass off, fast-tracking everything from high school to my law degree, so why would I handle the bar any differently?"

"You wouldn't." His father nodded. "And I would expect no less from my son."

No "well done, son." No "I'm proud of you." Max's fist tightened on the arm of the chair. Even if he became a carbon copy of his father, would it ever be enough?

"I'm eager to have you fully on board," his father went on to say. "We've been extremely busy, as you know, and it'll be good to have you finally ready to take on a load."

Jesus. Max's stomach roiled. His only interest in how the bar exam went was how it affected the firm's workload. He wasn't moving at his father's desired speed. His molars ached under the pressure of his jaw.

He stood. "Was that all?" he managed to ask through his teeth.

"No. Before you go…" His father opened one of his desk drawers. "Next month there's a charity event that we sponsor each year called Our Legacy Foundation." He pulled an envelope free. "I'm sure you've heard it mentioned before."

"I have," Max said.

"Something has come up, and your mother and I can't make the event. I thought this would be a good opportunity for you to represent the family and the business by going in our place." Maximo held out the envelope.

Reflex had Max accepting the tickets, despite the fact that he despised the spotlight. Especially when he would be alone in the spotlight. Alone and forced to deflect a multitude of questions from the guests, as well as the media, about the absence of a date on his arm.

However, like most things with his father, attending the event wasn't a request. It was an order.

"Of course, Father," he found himself saying.

"Good. Good," Maximo said. "I know you won't let us down."

"I'll handle it." Max slid the envelope into his pocket. "Anything else?"

"No." His father slipped on his glasses and turned to his PC, dismissing him. "When it comes to this event, I don't have to remind you of the discussion we've had about your private life, right?" he asked, his attention still fixed on his screen. "As long as it doesn't affect the company, we're good." He glanced up from over his readers. "You understand what I'm saying, son?"

Son? Give me a break.

The only time he ever used the term was when he wanted to make sure he'd driven home his point. Keep *it* out of the public eye. The "it" being the fact that Max was gay. Maximo didn't care that he slept with men as long as the media didn't get wind of it.

"Loud and clear," Max said, his tone devoid of emotion. Meeting complete, he headed for the door and exited the office.

Out in the hall, Max pressed his back against the closed door. Air rushed from his lungs as he palmed his midsection, attempting to suppress the hollow ache inside. He was such a dumbass for hoping that any discussion with his father would be different than the last. Each time he always ended up walking away with a big, fat stomachful of disappointment.

How many stomachaches would it take before he learned nothing would ever change?

• • •

The next several hours flew by. Probably because he'd dived into his work in an attempt to block the earlier conversation with his father from his mind. But before he knew it, Abbie was at his desk announcing the five o'clock hour.

"Thank God it's Friday," she said, wrapping an arm around his neck. "So, are we celebrating tonight?"

"Celebrating?" He slapped the last folder closed and stacked it in a bin.

"The bar is over. Oh my God…it feels like you have been doing nothing but taking exams for years. Aren't you relieved to finally be free?"

"Yes." He sighed. "You have no idea."

"Okay, so it's you, me, and a bottle of tequila tonight." A mischievous grin bloomed on his friend's mouth. "Come over later. We'll order a pizza, pick out a movie, do a few shots, and just relax. No worries about a designated driver. You can crash at my place."

He laughed. "You've thought of everything."

"You're my best friend, and you deserve a night without any stress."

He stood and loosened his tie. "It's Friday night, Abs. I'm sure you have better date options than a pizza, booze, and a gay man on your couch."

"I don't know what you mean? What could be any better than that?" She winked.

He shook his head. "You're a crazy woman."

His phone vibrated inside his pocket, and he tugged it free. The display read: *Can you talk?*

Patrick.

The world around him faded to gray, leaving only him and the phone in his hand. *Can you talk?* Max read the short message once more.

And again.

Talk about what?

"Max?"

In the distance, someone called his name.

"Max?"

He glanced up to find Abbie frowning.

"What? What's wrong?"

"Nothing's wrong," she said. "I was heading to my car and called out to you a couple of times." She looked at the phone in his hand. "Is everything okay?"

"I just need to call someone." He stuffed his cell back inside his pocket and started for the back exit.

"I thought you said you need to make a call." Confusion creased Abbie's brow.

"I will, on my way home." He wasn't about to call Patrick from the office. Whatever they had to talk about needed to be done in private.

She followed behind him. "Are we on for tonight?"

On his way out the door, he stopped, turned, and grasped the doorjamb. As attractive as her offer sounded, he truly just wanted to go home. "It was really sweet of you to invite me to hang. Especially on a Friday night, but —"

"But you want to go home." She laughed and shook her head. "How did I know you were going to say that?" She sighed.

He pulled her in for quick hug. "Because you know me so well. Thank you so much for the offer, though. Rain check?"

"Anytime," she said. "You know where to find me." She placed a kiss on his cheek before brushing past him, heading for her car. "See you Monday!'

"Don't drink all the tequila without me!" he called to her as she climbed into her Altima.

"No promises, baby." She grinned and slammed her door shut before cranking up the car and pulling away.

After tossing his blazer onto the passenger seat, Max pulled his phone from his pocket and settled into the car. Biting his bottom lip, he tapped the screen, preparing to reply to Patrick. But before he could respond, the phone lit up with a call coming in.

His mother.

They usually spoke at least once over the weekend, but her calling this early in the evening was odd.

He slid his finger along the display, answering, and placed the device to his ear.

"Hello, Mother."

"Max, love. How was your day?"

"It was fine. Is everything okay at home?" He started his car, needing some air inside the heated cabin, for more reasons than one. He loved his mother, but the way she tried to be the peacemaker drove him crazy. No matter how cold his father's behavior, she always made excuses for him.

"Oh, everything is fine. I talked to your father earlier, and he mentioned that you sat for your exams earlier this week."

"I did," he said. "And before you ask, I think it went well."

"That's wonderful! I'm so glad to hear it. I was thinking, I would love to have a family dinner to celebrate. How about this Sunday?"

"There's nothing to celebrate yet, Mother. My results won't be in until this fall."

"Well, I believe there is something to celebrate. You've worked hard, and this was the culmination of all that effort. We're very proud of you, darling."

"You mean *you're* very proud of me. Father is more impatient than proud. He's anxious to have his new attorney open for business." The ever-present sick feeling in the pit of his stomach festered at the mention of his earlier meeting with dear old Dad.

"Nonsense, Max. Your father is very proud. You know he's not one to express his sentiments about such things."

He sighed. "I know, Mother."

Claudia Segreti would never give up trying to make him believe that his father possessed a soft spot for his children. If it was there, then it was buried damn deep, because Max had never witnessed it.

"I know you want to believe that," he added.

"Because it's true. Your father loves you very much. He's only hard on you because he wants the best for you."

He could repeat the mantra word for word. It was the same speech his mother had been giving since he was in preschool.

"I'm not sure about Sunday," he said. God knew he had to change the subject or risk losing whatever he'd eaten for lunch.

"Oh…" she said, disappointment lacing the single word. "You know, Teresa Anne is home for the summer, and she's decided to stay. She's transferring to USC."

"That's great. I'd like to see her. But I'm going to have to pass on this Sunday. I'm sorry," he said, working his fist on the leather-wrapped steering wheel. "I just don't think it's a good idea." Having to sit across the table from his dad right now, before his results were in, sounded miserable. "Not yet," he added. "How about we wait until it's official that I've passed, so we'll truly have something to celebrate."

"If that's what you really want…"

"It is."

"We'll wait then, dear."

"Thanks, Mom. Tell Teresa I said hello, and that we'll get together soon. I'll call you later."

After they said their good-byes, Max ended the call. The message screen popped up where he'd left off. He studied it, a part of him curious to know what it was Patrick wanted to talk about. But the other half of him, the pissed-off half, wanted to make him wait.

He smirked. Shifting into reverse, he pulled out of the lot and into the rush hour traffic.

The pissed-off half had won.

Besides, he wasn't ready to deal with another stressful conversation on the heels of the last one.

Twenty-five minutes later, he entered his condo, the same one he'd lived in while at USC. His father kept the place on permanent family hold. He closed the door, flipped the switch for the lights, and made his way over to the island separating the kitchen from the living space. He tossed his keys and jacket onto the granite. Pulling his phone from his pocket, he brought up the message from Patrick. He typed one word in response: *yes*.

Max lowered the phone onto the stone and stared at the screen. After their last conversation, what was left to be said? He tugged his tie from around his neck and added it to the growing pile on his counter. Patrick had made it very clear how he felt about there being anything more between them than sex.

His cell buzzed with an incoming call, and Max's fingers froze on the buttons of his shirt.

Patrick.

"Here we go," he mumbled, picking up his phone. His stomach tightened as he answered. "Hello."

"Hey," Patrick said. "Thanks for taking my call."

Max wandered into the living room and settled onto the sofa. "What did you need to talk to me about?"

"I just wanted to thank you for helping us out with the attorney. He seems good, you know. Liam liked him, which was a major plus. And he was encouraging about my brother's record."

"That's good." Max picked at the lint clinging to his trousers. "I'm glad it worked out."

Patrick went on to ask him about how the bar exam went that week, congratulating him when Max told him he thought it went well.

The whole damn conversation could not have felt more strained and awkward.

"Not that I don't appreciate you asking me about my exams," Max said, the fingers of his free hand biting into the sofa's leather armrest. "But I get the feeling that's not what you called me about."

Being the son of one of the best trial attorneys in the state, it was odd that he despised confronting a person on sensitive topics. But law school helped him to push past the fear in most situations—except for when it came to his father. Confronting Maximo Sr. was on a whole different phobia level, one that no amount of graduate school could tackle.

"You're right. That wasn't the only thing I called about," Patrick said. "I wasn't… We didn't… I guess what I'm trying to say is that I didn't exactly handle things the greatest. You know, when we last saw each other."

"You think?"

"I was kind of an asshole."

Max clamped his lower lip with his teeth. Patrick said it, not him. But he wasn't going to deny it. "Yeah, you were."

"Thanks," he grunted.

"But you weren't totally off base. My family would

probably feel that way about where we come from—our differences. But I'm not them."

"Okay," Patrick said. "I hear you."

"A lot's changed since USC."

"You're telling me," Patrick said. "I've got the scars to prove it."

"But we're still the same two people who connected over drinks back then."

"I can't agree with you there, Blue Eyes."

"You're wrong," he said.

Patrick scoffed. "Tell me how you really feel."

"Are you too chicken? Is that what this is?" What the hell was he doing baiting PG? This was so not him. He didn't play games with guys. Hell, he barely gave any guy the time of day, much less taunted them into a date.

"What?" Patrick laughed, and it was the sexiest damn thing he'd ever heard. "Me? Chicken?"

"Yep. I call it how I see it. You're just too damn chicken to actually ask me out."

A low groan rumbled over the phone line. "You're playing with fire, Segreti."

"Maybe," Max said. "But I'm all grown up now, and I know how to handle it."

"Fine," Patrick said. "Since we're both adults, meet me for a drink tonight."

"Are you asking me, or telling me?"

"Which would you prefer?" The deep sound of his voice washed over Max like warm chocolate liqueur.

Decadent.

Heady. And laced with a promise to fulfill all his wicked desires.

"Where do you want to meet?"

Chapter Ten

This was a terrible idea.

Patrick motioned for the bartender to hit him again with another round. Maybe this shot would begin to dull the panic growing in his nervous system, buzzing inside his head like a hive of angry bees. What had he been thinking, inviting Max to Proclivity tonight?

He eyed the front door for probably the one-hundredth time in the last fifteen minutes. Still no sign of him yet. Glancing up at the bar's mirror, he took in the dark burgundy and black of the booths, tables, and floor. The deep bass of the music reverberated from the speakers and vibrated through his chest, the beat perfect for fucking.

A couple stood from one of the booths, drawing his attention. With their drinks in hand, they headed toward the rear of the club and the private rooms. Speaking of fucking…

He palmed his refilled shot glass and slammed the tequila to the back of his throat. The burn slithered down his esophagus and bloomed in his chest. *Christ.* He groaned.

This was a terrible idea.

Proclivity was where he went when he needed a nameless, no-strings-attached release. A haven, where for a couple of hours he was in control. A place where he could privately exorcise his demons, his frustrations.

So why in hell had he invited Max to walk through those doors for a glimpse of his dark side?

Movement near the front captured his attention, drawing him out of his thoughts. Max stood by the entrance, speaking to the bouncer. The dark waves of his short hair were perfectly groomed as always, but tonight instead of dressing the part of a junior executive, Max wore a black leather jacket. The cowhide fit his torso like a fucking glove, and below that, he'd pulled on a pair of gray, shredded jeans that hugged his thighs and ass. Patrick's cock swelled, hardening in approval.

Holy fuck.

When had the guy learned to dress like that? Better question, who had taught his nerd to dress like that?

His nerd? An alarm went off inside his head. Those two words sounded too damn possessive. And getting possessive spelled danger. Not for the other guy, but for himself. For his ability to survive one more loss in his life, if his brother's prediction about him and Max proved correct.

Patrick slid from his bar stool and made his way over. Closing in on the bouncer, Patrick nodded in Max's direction. "He's with me."

"Yes, sir," the bouncer said. "Have a nice evening."

"Thanks, Joe," Patrick said, and glanced over to Max. "Ready for that drink?" he asked, lifting a brow. The signal had been subtle, but judging by the smirk on the other man's face, Max had caught and understood his warning: *this is your last chance to run.*

"More than ready," Max said.

"Okay, then. Follow me." Patrick led the way back to the bar and selected two seats at the far end of the polished mahogany. Max slid onto the stool beside him.

Motioning for the bartender, Patrick glanced over at his date. Damn, the moment was almost surreal. "I wasn't sure if you were going show."

"I said I would."

"I know. But this isn't exactly Bernie's." Patrick smirked as the bartender approached.

Max's brows lifted, and he glanced around. "Bernie's it is not."

"Beer?" Patrick asked.

"That sounds fine."

"Two beers, please," Patrick said to the tall, bald barkeep. He nodded and headed off. "You know, I think this is the first time I've known you to have a drink."

"I don't do alcohol often," Max said. "I'm usually too busy studying or catching up on work. I can't risk being unable to focus."

The bartender arrived and placed the bottle on the counter. Patrick grabbed his and raised it in Max's direction. "Here's to a night of freedom, where you don't have to think at all."

Max reached for his beer, lifted it, and clinked the glass with Patrick's. "Are you offering to do it for me?"

"Me...think for you?"

Blue Eyes smiled and took a swig of his beer.

"Now there's a scary thought." Patrick chuckled and turned his bottle up to his lips.

"I don't know," Max began. "It might be fun to see what you'd do with me if I were in your hands."

Beer stalled in Patrick's throat, his head swimming as every drop of blood rushed to his cock at the thought of Max on his knees, willingly submissive to his every fantasy. Forcing his mind back to reality, Patrick swallowed hard and searched for his voice. "You think so, huh?"

Max laughed and took another swig from his beer. His Adam's apple bobbed, and Patrick couldn't help but watch, mesmerized by the up and down motion of his throat. How would it feel gliding hot and tight over the head of his dick?

"Patrick…" Max called out.

"I'm sorry." He shook his head, trying to focus. "Did you say something?"

"I asked how long you've been a member here."

"Oh, since I was with the Packers."

"I take it the place is welcoming to gay, straight, and everything else in the spectrum," Max said, scanning the room and its patrons.

"Whatever gets you off." *And you get me off so fucking hard,* he wanted to say. But the words sat frozen on his tongue, immobilized by something he didn't want to put a label on. Because if he had to look at it too long, he was pretty damn sure he'd see fear. And he hated cowards.

Patrick picked up his beer and stood. "Let's find a spot that's more comfortable."

"Sounds good." Max snagged his bottle, slid from his seat, and followed close behind him.

Near the back, Patrick spotted an open booth. *Perfect.* He couldn't help but smile as he maneuvered into the half circle, which faced a viewing window at a perfect angle. Moving farther into the booth, he made room for Max to join him.

Max plopped his beer onto the small round table and settled onto the seat. The area in the back was dimly lit. The only light came from a small candle inside a glass orb on the center of their table and the glow through the glass of the two interior windows in front of them.

Patrick knew the moment Max had caught sight of the show. His breath hitched, and his spine pressed into the back of the booth.

Closing the gap between them, Patrick slipped his arm

onto the top of the booth and around Max. His thigh brushed Max's as he pressed his chest against the other man's arm and whispered near Max's ear. "Do you like to watch?"

"I…" Max's mouth clamped shut, and he snatched his beer from the table for a large gulp. Finished, he plopped it back on the wood before continuing. "I've never." He shook his head.

"You've watched porn before, right?" Patrick reached around and flattened his palm over Max's midsection, soaking up the warmth radiating from his body.

"That's different, and you know it."

Following Max's line of sight, Patrick took in the couple on display. A tall bear of a man dressed in leather chaps stood with his bare ass facing the glass. His cheeks flexed as he plowed over and over into his willing male partner, bent over a bench. Each hard surge of his hips sent his cub's heels lifting from the floor. But judging by the dazed expression of pleasure on his bottom's face, he was loving every minute of it.

Patrick flicked his gaze to the man at his side. Even in the dim room, the heat in Max's face was easy to see. "You're right. Voyeurism is very different from the staged porn on your TV."

"Are you trying to shock me, Patrick?"

Was he? Was that why he'd invited him? Patrick slid his hand lower, brushing the hard outline of Max's cock before settling on his thigh. But he hadn't missed his date's sharp inhale. "What if I was?"

"Then I'd tell you…" Max glanced up from under his lashes. "It's not working," he whispered. "I'm not scared of you." Max's hand covered the back of his.

"You should be." He pulled his arm back.

"Why?" Max twisted in his seat, putting them face-to-face.

"Because this won't end well," he stated, his voice hushed, but firm.

"Because you say so?"

Dammit! Why was he pushing this? "Because I'm not what you need." That was the fucking truth. Max deserved someone in his life who didn't screw up everything he touched. He hadn't been able to save his career or his father.

Max palmed the back of Patrick's head, pulling him closer. "I already have a father trying to run my life. I don't need another. So why don't you let me decide who or what I need."

His mouth crushed against Patrick's, demanding, nipping at his lower lip. Patrick's blood heated, the fire coursing through his veins, burning him up. *Fuck.* Unable to resist another second, he opened, inviting him inside. Their tongues dueled, battling for dominance, each too hungry to allow the other to lead. The tip of Max's tongue flicked against the roof of Patrick's mouth, teasing him, brushing the sensitive surface before thrusting deep once more. Patrick groaned. It was too much, yet not nearly enough.

Driving his fingers into Max's hair, Patrick held him in place as he lifted his lashes, and his date stared back at him, his blue eyes clouded, drunk with desire. Patrick's cock pulsed with each pounding beat of his heart. Had he ever wanted another man this much?

It was a stupid, rhetorical question.

He knew the answer. And it was *hell to the fucking no*.

Problem was, what the hell was he supposed to do about it? He'd already proven to himself that once was not enough with the man.

But a relationship?

He wasn't a relationship kind of guy. Didn't have the time or space in his life for romance.

With his thumb Patrick traced the outline of the other

man's freshly shaven jaw, stopping beneath the sensual curve of his lower lip. Max's mouth parted, and the warmth of his sigh enveloped Patrick's fingertip. Instinct had him thrusting the end of his thumb between his lips. Max closed around him, his tongue exploring Patrick's flesh before he proceeded to suck the tip. Each pull of his mouth resonated straight through the head of dick. Unbidden, Patrick's eyelids lowered. His head swam, buzzed on lust.

And at that moment he couldn't fathom any damn reason why he hadn't made Max his.

Curling his fingers into the other guy's hair, Patrick tugged his thumb free. *Damn, what a shame.* He groaned. The man had a fucking gorgeous mouth, and he intended to put it to better use.

"I want you," Patrick growled.

"Here?" Max tugged at Patrick's shirt, his fingertips exploring the section of abs he'd bared.

The idea of taking him to one of the back rooms of Proclivity like another anonymous hookup made his gut roil. He frowned.

"No," he said. "Not here. Not ever here."

"Okay," Max said. "What do you want to do?"

That was the question, wasn't it? Running the pad of his thumb once more over Max's full lower lip, the decision was clear. He couldn't go another night without him.

"There's a motel about a mile and a half south of here." Patrick released his hold, took another swig of his beer, and glanced back at his date. "If that's what you want?"

Max nodded. "I'll be there."

The trip to the hotel might as well have been twenty miles instead of less than two, judging by the ache in his balls. After securing a room for the night, Patrick made his way down the hall, Max following close behind him. He shoved the keycard into the slot and a green light flashed on the lock. Palming the handle, he opened the door and stepped aside, allowing Max to enter.

How had he survived three long years without being inside the guy again?

Patrick snagged his arm, yanking him back around.

"Come here," he rumbled right before he pressed Max's shoulders against the wall. The door clanked shut as Patrick seized Max's wrists and pulled them over his head. "I'm going to taste every inch of you."

"Fuck, yes," he muttered, surging his hips into Patrick's. "I want…"

He traced the seam of his lover's lips with his tongue. "Tell me what you want."

"You," he breathed, and tugged against the hold on his wrists. "You. Everywhere."

His pulse roaring inside his head, Patrick brushed his mouth over Max's. "That's exactly what I'm going to give you, baby." He pressed his lips to Max's once more, and this time he forced himself to slow down. To lick and sample every corner, every nuance. To make love to his mouth.

A moan rose from Max's throat. "You're killing me."

Lowering his arms, Patrick released Max's wrists. "You've got way too many clothes on." He slipped his hands under the other guy's jacket, removing it from his shoulders.

"That makes two of us," Max said. He grabbed a handful of Patrick's shirt, yanking it over his head. "Much better." His gaze raked Patrick's torso.

"You like what you see?" Patrick smirked.

"The view just keeps getting better and better." Max went for the zipper and button to Patrick's jeans, but he blocked him.

"You have some catching up to do," he said, his brows lifting. "Take it off, Blue Eyes." Patrick backed away. He wanted the best view in the house for the show. He dropped onto the hotel's plush chair and finished opening his fly. His cock sprang free, rock hard and resting on his lower abs. He spread his legs in silent invitation.

Tossing his boots to the side, Max sauntered farther into the room, following his lead. Stopping in front of Patrick's knees, he tugged his shirt over his head then dropped it to the floor by his feet. Patrick fisted his hands on his thighs. He had to, or he'd end up grabbing the sexy nerd and finishing what he'd started against the wall.

"Now this is voyeurism at its best," Patrick said instead. "You, alone with me, getting naked."

Max smiled, sliding his palms down his own chest, over the fine trail of hairs that vanished beneath his waistband. He eased the button to his fly open. "I'm glad you like."

"Oh yeah." Patrick nodded, his cock already wet, resting against his skin. "I like." *Shit.* He wasn't going to last long. Not the first round, at least. Blue Eyes may not realize yet, but he had every intention of fucking him more than once before letting him out of there.

The zipper on Max's jeans made a popping sound as he tugged downward on the tab. Rocking his hips, Max worked the denim lower until it fell around his ankles, revealing a black pair of boxer briefs. The erection hiding behind the cotton pressed against the material, forming a beautiful, thick outline, one that had Patrick's mouth watering. *Holy fuck.*

"Show me," Patrick uttered, his voice deep, guttural.

He stepped out of his jeans then hooked his thumbs under the waistband of his briefs, dragging them down before tossing both items aside. As he straightened, Max's cock jutted out, fully erect, the head flushed a darker shade than the shaft. Patrick's own erection bucked at the sight.

Leaning forward in his chair, he cupped the other man's ass, holding him steady, as he used the tip of his tongue to sample the droplet of pre-cum. Max hissed, and a fine tremor shook his frame. The flavor rolled over Patrick's taste buds, drawing a moan from the back of his throat.

Patrick pushed to his feet and walked Max backward toward the bed. The law grad lowered himself onto the side of the mattress, his attention fixed on Patrick's every move. Patrick toed off his boots, pulled from his pocket the condoms and lube he'd grabbed before exiting his car, and finished shedding his jeans. He nudged the other guy's knees apart, inserting himself between them. "I keep my promises," he growled, lowering himself over Max.

"I do like that in a man." The back of Max's head bumped the comforter as Patrick braced himself with his palms, hovering mere inches above him.

"You're going to like this even more, baby." Patrick found the throbbing pulse at Max's neck with his lips. Leaving a trail of wet, open mouth kisses in his wake, Patrick reacquainted himself with every inch of the other man from his throat down his torso to the hot tip of his cock. Around and around, he circled the flushed rim, lapping up each drop of pre-cum.

Panting, Max writhed under his ministrations. "Fuck…" He clawed at Patrick's biceps. "Take it. Come on. Need your mouth."

Instead, working from the seam separating his balls, Patrick licked his way upward. Holding Max's shaft steady with his fist, Patrick dragged the flat surface of his tongue north along the backside of his erection.

"Christ…" Max's hips bucked.

Beneath the crown, Patrick stroked the sensitive flesh with his tongue.

"Yes…fuck." Max groaned. "Patrick…"

Damn, he loved the way the nerd moaned his name. Geez, how idiotic was that?

"I'm going crazy here, man." Max's head thrashed against the bed. "I need to come."

Patrick ran his arms beneath the other man's knees, pushing his legs up and back, exposing Max's backside. "When I'm inside you, then you can come. Not before."

Squeezing his eyelids shut, Max groaned, "Oh, damn. That has to be the hottest thing I've ever heard."

"Hold your legs," Patrick ordered. Max opened his eyes and complied. "I'm not finished tasting you yet." Patrick massaged his palms over Max's smooth cheeks. "God, you have a gorgeous ass." His own hard-on twitched as if in agreement.

Leaning in closer, he laved his tongue over the area between his sac and hole.

"Fuck," Max spat. "So good."

Inch by inch, Patrick worked his way toward Max's tight ring. Slowly, he circled the other man's hole until he reached the center. He pressed the tip inside at the same time that he reached up and fisted Max's cock. A gasp from his lover reached his ears. The other man opened, allowing him deeper. In and out, he fucked Max with his tongue while his fist stroked the other man's stiff shaft. He'd never been much into going down on another guy's backdoor. But with Max… For some reason he was different. There wasn't a part of him that Patrick didn't want to mark, taste—hell, claim.

"Patrick!" Max bucked hard beneath him. "Jesus, you have to…" His breath hitched. "Too good." He groaned. "I'm going to come if you don't stop."

Pulling away, Patrick glanced up. "Not yet," he said, his voice gravelly. "Not without me." Patrick snatched the condom from where he'd left it on the nightstand, tore the wrapper with his teeth, and pulled it free. Gritting his teeth, he rolled the latex over his sensitized flesh. "Dammit," he chewed out. "I don't know how slow I'm going to be able take this." His balls were already on fire, and his control was slipping. "I'm too close to the edge."

"Don't you fucking dare go slow," Max barked.

After applying a generous amount of lube to his shaft, Patrick nudged the head of his cock against Max's entrance.

"Fuck, yes," Max said. "Do it."

Patrick closed his eyes, searching for every last ounce of his control. He couldn't lose it like a teenager. On a deep breath, he surged inside. Max's tight heat enveloped his shaft like a fucking glove, short-circuiting his mind.

"Jesus!" Max gasped. "Too much." He hissed, losing his grip on his knees to fist the comforter at his sides. "Burning."

Dammit. "Need me to stop?" He bit out the words. He'd fucking die if he had to, but for Max, he'd find the strength.

"No." Max panted. "Need you."

"I got you, baby." Clutching the other guy's legs, he pushed them back, giving him better access. He eased out until only the head of his shaft remained inside. "Wrap your hand around your cock," Patrick said. Max curled his fist around his length. "That's right. Stroke it for me." He plunged back inside, clamping down on his molars as his balls drew tight. Too fucking soon. Max groaned, working the end of his cock. "Show me how good it feels to have me inside you."

Patrick pumped his hips. The sound of their slapping together over and over again filled the room. *More.*

Deeper.

Harder. The base of his spine tingled, signaling the cusp of his orgasm. Fuck. It was right there. Air burst in and out of his chest. Not yet. His pace faltered. Not yet. He needed for Max to come first, needed to watch as pleasure washed over his face. Pleasure that he was responsible for.

"Come for me, Blue Eyes," he rasped.

"Patrick," Max groaned, and his eyelids lifted.

"Let me see you come."

Rocking his hips, he thrust his cock deep, over and over, giving him every inch. All of him.

"Oh fuck." Max gasped, his body jerking in time with the impact of Patrick's hips. "Fuck, yes!" His back bowed, jets of cum painting his chest. "Oh, God…" he grunted. "Patrick."

Like a gate on his orgasm had been blasted open by the sight and sounds of his lover's release, cum raced up his shaft and exploded from the tip. "Max," he cried out.

Pulse after pulse of ecstasy pumped from his balls, filling his condom. A hard tremor rocked his body. *Fuck.* Releasing his hold on Max's legs, he fell forward, catching himself with his hands. Still flying high, hard pants rushing from his lungs, he closed his eyes, trying to focus on calming his heart rate. Damn, he could hardly catch his breath.

Warm fingertips brushed his cheeks and slid into his hair. Patrick opened his eyes. The glassy look in Max's gaze told him it hadn't been long since he'd fallen back to earth. Patrick's cock twitched, still half hard and buried inside his lover.

"Damn, PG," Max said, his voice raw, rusty.

"Yeah…" It was all he could manage while he spun back down from his trip into the pleasure zone known as Max. Lowering his head, he brushed Max's mouth with his. He had to have one more taste. "That was fucking off the charts," he muttered next to his lips.

Hell, after that, the charts would have to be renamed.

Redefined.

"You're telling me," Max said.

His shaft slid free from his lover, and Patrick rolled onto the bed beside him, their labored breaths the only sound in the room.

When was the last time he'd shared a hotel room with someone and hadn't felt like running the moment after he'd found his release? Hell, he couldn't remember. Probably never. Glancing at his lover, he perused Max's flushed cheeks, his chest rising and falling, the surface streaked with the evidence of his orgasm. His mouth watered with the sudden urge to sample every drop. His shaft flexed at the thought. Damn, he already wanted him again. The dude was like crack to him.

And he was so fucking lost, with no rehab in sight.

Worse, he was pretty sure that curing his addiction was the last thing he wanted.

Chapter Eleven

I missed you.

Max stared at Patrick's sleeping profile and the way his long, thick lashes brushed the delicate flesh beneath his eyes. The three words echoed inside his head. But he didn't dare let them out.

Last night had been surreal.

Fucking awesome.

Yet something inside warned him that Patrick was still on the edge, skittish about things getting too serious. That Patrick believed anything between them beyond a few hot rolls in the sack would be impossible. Hell, maybe he was right.

His stomach twisted at the thought.

But what if he was wrong?

He tightly curled his fingers, doing his best to quell the sudden desire to run his fingertips along the shadow of the other man's beard and feel the coarse bristles scratch his skin. Max swallowed hard. He couldn't take the chance of history repeating itself—of having to watch him walk away again. And this time might be forever.

From that first evening they'd spent together, Max had had a feeling no one would ever compare to Patrick. And he'd been right.

PG was a force of nature. Unique. Tough as hell. Yet he also had a vulnerable side that drew him like a moth to a flame. But Max didn't give a shit if he got burned as long as he was flying close to his light, touching him, catching a glimpse of his heart.

As if Patrick had heard his thoughts, the big guy opened his eyes. He blinked and glanced Max's way. "Hey there," Patrick said, a sleepy smile curling the corners of his mouth.

"Hey, sleepyhead," Max replied. Finally giving in to the need to reach, to touch, he ran his palm along Patrick's cheek

"Wow." Patrick surged up onto his elbow, his focus trained on the beam of sunlight that had found the opening between the hotel's drapes. "What time is it?"

Max rolled onto his side, scanning the nightstand. "If that clock is right, it's seven thirty."

"I should be getting home." Patrick sighed, dropped onto the pillow, and shoved back the hair on his forehead. "I don't want Liam to wake up and find out that I'm not home."

"He's a teenager, I bet he sleeps late on the weekend."

"Shit. That's right. It's Saturday." He looked Max's way and smiled. "That would mean I do have a little more time." Patrick draped his arm over Max and closed the distance between them. Max's morning wood pressed into Patrick's hard abs as the other man's erection nudged Max's upper thigh. "What do you think we should do with the next hour before we have to return the world? I know what I'm voting for."

His smile morphing from amused to wicked, Patrick slung his leg over Max's, and his hand slid south and cupped Max's ass.

Max chuckled. "I do like where your mind is heading."

Patrick growled and rocked his hard shaft into Max's leg. "That's not my mind, baby. Although…" The sharp edge of Patrick's teeth nipped Max's shoulder right before he soothed the sting with his tongue. "I am having some very dirty thoughts involving you and me that are driving me crazy right now."

A warm feeling ignited in Max's center at the mental images Patrick inspired. The feeling arrowed straight to his shaft, bringing him to a rock-hard state. "How about we take a shower and you demonstrate a few of those?"

Patrick lifted his head, facing him. "I always said you were a smart guy." He rolled away and stood.

"So you've been talking about me, huh?" Max winked.

A chuckle sounded, and Patrick strode bare-assed toward the bathroom. Damn, the sight of his nude backside was nearly enough to stop Max's heart. From his broad shoulders to his narrow waist and lower to his strong thighs and tight calves, the guy was a living and breathing lesson in Greek sculpture.

He disappeared into the other room, and Max shook himself out of his daze. The sound of water hitting the tiles in the shower had him scrambling off the bed to join him.

Inside the bathroom, Max stopped at the counter to drink in the view. Patrick was already on the other side of the glass shower doors, his body wet, glistening with droplets of water. Fuck, he could've stood there all day watching Patrick under the shower spray. Maybe he *was* into voyeurism.

"Don't tell me I'm going to have to soap myself?" Patrick peered through the glass, pushing his damp hair back over his forehead.

"No way, man." Max frowned. "Total injustice, having to lather all that alone."

"That's what I'm saying…"

Max slid the door back, stepped into the tub, and closed the glass behind him. Patrick grinned and tossed him a bottle of shower gel. He snagged it from the air with one hand. Oh, yeah. He didn't have to be asked twice.

After squeezing some of the fruity smelling product into his palm, Max closed in on his lover.

"I'll try to be gentle," he said, schooling his expression as he spread the soap over the other guy's pecs.

"Now why the hell would you want to do that?"

Glancing up, Max found a devilish gleam in Patrick's hazel eyes. His hands covered the backs of Max's.

"I'm yours, Blue Eyes," Patrick said, his voice raspy. "Right here. Right now. I'm yours. Whatever you want."

Steam swirled around them, yet a shiver raced over Max's flesh. Not even in his fantasies had he dared to dream a moment like this one. "Whatever I want?"

Patrick clamped Max's face between his palms, holding him steady. "Anything," he breathed, droplets of water clinging to his lashes.

Inside, Max was dying to ask him to never let go. To demand he freeze time so they could stay like this forever. God, how he wanted to forget about their reality. Instead, he massaged Patrick's shoulders, building the lather. "Put your hands on the wall," Max ordered.

His eyebrows kicking up, Patrick grunted, but did as instructed.

If Patrick was handing over the reins of control, dammit, he was determined to make the most of what few minutes they had left together.

Roaming lower, Max flicked his fingers over the other male's nipples. Patrick's breath hitched. "You like that." Max smirked.

A grunt was his lover's only response.

He circled the dark, taut buds, then squeezed the sensitive flesh. Patrick's body tensed. His biceps flexed as his cock jerked, rising between them toward Patrick's abs.

"So responsive." Max moaned. "I'll have to file that away."

His eyelids narrowing over a storm of brown and green, Patrick's gaze honed in on Max's. "Be careful. Teasing a wild animal is never a good idea."

"You gonna bite me, PG?" Max licked his lips.

Patrick's fingers curled against tile.

"So hard, baby," he growled. "And you'll like it."

Oh, fuck. He bet he would. Max's balls tightened. Could a guy come from a visual image inspired by words alone?

"You know what I want?" Max slid his hands lower, his fingertips cresting and dipping into the hills and valleys of Patrick's abs. Patrick's cock twitched as if in anticipation of Max's arrival. "I want to make you come."

Wrapping his fingers around the other man's thick girth, Max worked his slick palm over Patrick's cock, wringing a hiss from his lover.

"I want to be the one who makes you lose control." Max kneeled on the wet surface.

Patrick shook his head, dark red strands of hair clinging to his face. "You already are, baby," he rasped, the words barely above a whisper.

But Max heard them. The four words detonated inside him, rocking his core and giving him a high like no drug could have ever managed.

Max tightened his grip on the other man's erection and slid his palm from root to tip. Patrick's head lolled between his shoulders. With his free hand, Max cupped the weight of his lover's balls. Tugging on the sac, Max slowly pumped Patrick's shaft, working it with a corkscrew action. Patrick groaned, a throaty sound that said he approved. And nothing had ever sounded hotter.

He worked his hand back up toward the head of his cock, paying special attention to the sensitive spot on the backside.

"Fuck," Patrick gasped. "Faster, baby." He rocked his hips,

trying to force his cock through Max's fist.

A droplet of pre-cum swelled in the slit and spilled over. Max groaned, his mouth watering at the sight. "Hang on, big guy," he said. "I'm going to take you there. Promise."

Rolling his head on his shoulders, Patrick groaned.

"Let me in." Max nudged at Patrick's thighs, and he spread his legs a little wider. Max slid a hand farther back, massaging the space between Patrick's sac and opening.

"Max," Patrick bit out, pumping his hips hard.

Oh, yeah. He liked that.

Max picked up the pace, stroking his lover's cock faster. Using the fingertips of his other hand, he circled Patrick's tight rim. "You want me there, big guy?"

"Fuck, yes," he panted. "I want." Patrick hissed, hips bucking "Faster. Need it. Fuck. Need you."

Max pressed his slick index finger against his lover's tight ring. Patrick opened, and he slipped inside.

Patrick cursed. "Max. Fuck…Max."

His cock swelled, thickened inside Max's palm. He pumped faster, twisting his fist over the length.

"Fuck me, Max!" Patrick arched, bucked. "Dammit. Don't stop."

No way in hell. Adding another finger inside him, Max worked both digits in and out while his other hand stroked the end of Patrick's rod.

"That's it." Patrick grunted. "Fuck." He panted. "Going to come."

He was magnificent, and Max was transfixed. He'd never felt more alive than at that moment, knowing he was responsible for the pleasure engulfing the hard, gorgeous man in front of him.

Bowing over, Patrick cried out. Cum splattered Max's chest. "Max…" He glanced up, his eyes glassy. "Holy shit. Still coming."

"I got you." Max continued to pump him, draining every

drop he could squeeze.

Several seconds later, Patrick captured Max's nape with one hand. Max looked up as he dragged a finger through the cum on his chest. He placed the digit between his lips, and the salty-sweet flavor of his lover exploded over his taste buds. Max's cock pulsed, ached from the need to give up his own release. He moaned, and Patrick's gaze turned dark, wicked.

"Stand up," Patrick commanded.

Max pulled his fingers free and stood. His shaft bobbed heavy between his legs.

"Mine," the big guy said a second before he dropped to his knees, pressing Max against the tile. One moment, Patrick had Max's length in his fist, and the next, the head of his erection bumped the back of his lover's throat. Air punched from Max's lungs from the overload of sensation. His head thumped against the tiles. Patrick swallowed, and the muscles along his throat massaged the end of Max's shaft.

"Jesus!" Max gasped. His balls tightened, sending a bolt of pleasure up his spine. "Patrick!" He scrambled for a fistful of the guy's hair.

His lover's head reared back on a needy inhale, his tongue dragging along the back of Max's shaft. And the orgasm caught Max by surprise.

Black dots spiraled in his vision. His knees weakened. On and on it seemed his orgasm pumped up his length. When the pleasure became too much, Max pulled his softening erection free.

"No more," he groaned. "You got everything."

"Not nearly enough yet." The big guy worked his way up Max's body, tasting, licking a path north to his face. Once there, he sealed his mouth over Max's. The kiss was desperate, as if Patrick were the devil and Max was his one chance for salvation. But Patrick had it all wrong.

He was the one saving him.

Chapter Twelve

Walk of shame…meet Patrick Guinness.

Wasn't that what it was called when someone found himself creeping through the back door after being out all night, hoping that his brother was still asleep? Yet, instead of feeling remorse or embarrassment about who and what he'd done, Patrick couldn't seem to wipe the smile off his face.

What the hell?

Patrick dragged his palm over his mouth and jaw, attempting to erase the unfamiliar sensation. Since when did he start allowing himself to get all mushy over a guy?

Inside the house, he listened for any telltale signs that Liam was awake. But the house was quiet. *Thank God.* He wasn't ready to face any questions from his brother about where he'd been all night.

He dropped his keys in the basket on the kitchen counter, washed his hands, and targeted the fridge. As if the sight of the white box had awakened his gut, Patrick's stomach growled. Damn, he couldn't remember the last time he'd eaten. Yanking open the door, he savored the cold, dry air washing over him.

He breathed deep, taking the chill to his lungs. Between the energetic hours he'd spent with Max, and the brutal South Carolina summer, his body temp felt pegged out.

He spotted a carton of eggs plus a package of bacon, and his mouth watered. That should do the trick. Not to mention how surprised Liam would be to wake up to the smell of breakfast. Another grin tugged at his mouth. It had been way too long since he and his brother had shared something other than a bowl of cold cereal or a Pop-Tart in the morning.

Twenty minutes later, Patrick was in heaven from the smell of fried bacon wafting throughout the kitchen.

"What the hell is going on in here?" Liam appeared in the entrance to the bedroom hallway.

Patrick glanced up from the stove. "Breakfast." He popped a piece of the crispy meat into his mouth. "Has it been so long since you've smelled bacon that you're confused?"

"No." Liam strode farther into the room. "It's the sight of you over the stove frying it up that's blowing my mind." The younger Guinness stared at the pan of scrambled eggs and draining slices of the fried pork. "What's gotten into you?" His expression twisted. "Wait." Liam shook his head and held up his palm. "I don't want to know."

"What are you talking about?" Patrick pushed the skillet off the burner and flicked off the knob controlling the flame. "I'm hungry, and I wanted to make us a good breakfast. You know, do something crazy, like you and me sharing a hot meal." He shrugged.

Liam grabbed a couple of slices of bread, a plate, and proceeded to help himself. "No. You're trying to make up for the fact that you never came home last night." Without looking back, he marched toward the table and plopped down on one of the chairs. Scooping up some of the eggs along with the bacon, Liam folded them inside a slice of bread. He glanced over at Patrick before adding, "Those are the same clothes you had on when you left here." His brother shoved a corner of the sandwich into his mouth.

The little shit… Who the hell does he think he is calling me out like I'm a kid caught sneaking in after curfew?

Patrick would tell him to piss off if he weren't feeling so guilty about not being there through the night. After their dad died, he'd tried to do everything possible to make sure Liam felt like he had a stable home. Someone that would always be there for him, day and night.

"Listen, I'm sorry about—"

"Stop," Liam said. "I don't want to know who you were with, or what you were doing." He frowned. "For Christ's sake, spare me. I don't have to be a psychic to guess who you hooked up with last night." He rolled his eyes, palmed the rest of his breakfast, and left his seat.

"Fine." Patrick gritted his teeth. "I wouldn't dare make you suffer any more than you have to."

Liam grunted and brushed past him. "I gotta go to work."

"Work?" Patrick spun, following his brother through the kitchen. *What the hell?* "When did you get a job?"

"Yesterday." Liam swiped his keys from the counter. "I had an interview at McDonald's. The one near I-77. I wasn't sure if the guy was going to give me a chance with everything that's going down. But I thought it couldn't hurt to try. And if I got the job…" Liam looked back at him. "It would be a start, you know?"

A knot formed at the base of Patrick's throat. Maybe his baby brother was finally growing up. "I'm proud of you, Liam."

"Yeah, well." His brother shrugged. "I'll just be flipping burgers, not running the country."

Patrick chuckled. "One day."

"Ah, hell no." Liam shook his head. "You couldn't pay me enough to be responsible for all this shit." He headed for the back door.

"Hey, wait!"

Liam halted.

"I've got something for you." Patrick grabbed his keys from the basket and tossed them at his brother. Liam snatched them from the air.

"Seriously?" His eyebrows shot up. "You're going to let me drive your truck?"

"I'm not going anywhere for a while, since Tommie's got the shop for the weekend. Besides, I've got my bike if something comes up. Think you can handle something bigger than that Escort?"

"Hell, yeah." A grin busted his face.

Damn, he missed seeing the kid smile.

"Just bring it back in one piece." Patrick snagged a strip of bacon. "And without any extra dents!" he managed to yell as the door slammed shut behind his brother.

After filling himself up with most of what was left of the breakfast he'd prepared, Patrick climbed into bed to get a few extra hours of shut-eye. But after two hours of tossing and turning, reliving every minute of the night before with Max behind his eyelids, he couldn't take it anymore.

"I gotta get out of here," he mumbled to himself.

He dragged on a pair of blue jeans over his boxer briefs, stuffed his feet into a pair of boots, and pulled on an Aerosmith graphic tee. The band wasn't exactly his generation, but his dad had loved them and always had their music blasting in the shop. According to their father, there was no way his kids were growing up without an appreciation for the eighties. And yeah, Patrick thought on the way out of his bedroom, Steven Tyler still rocked.

In the kitchen, he dug out the keys for his bike from the basket on the counter. This was exactly what he needed. He couldn't wait to feel the bike humming between his legs and the wind blasting over him. Patrick strode out the house, locking the door behind him.

Outside in the small, detached garage, he snagged his helmet from a hook near his bike and shoved the obsidian globe onto his head. Grabbing the handlebars to the motorcycle, he swung a leg over his red and black Ducati Superbike, the one luxury item he still possessed from his NFL days. Like an idiot, he'd blown a lot of his money in those first few months after signing, but his bike wasn't one of his regrets.

Patrick pressed the start button, and his ride roared to life. A grin tugged at his mouth, and his pulse edged higher. His crotch rocket had acquired a few scratches and dings over the past couple of years, so trying to sell it would be a waste of time for the amount of money it would bring. Which he had to admit, didn't break his heart.

He rolled out of the garage and headed for the open road. Breathing deep, he accelerated. Maybe after a couple of hours on two wheels going nowhere in particular, he could clear his head, and push a certain nerd to the back of his mind.

Gearing down, he lowered his torso into the wind.

If only he could get the little voice inside his skull—the one that kept whispering "you're fooling yourself"—to shut up.

Sometime around midafternoon, Patrick rolled his motorcycle to a stop and pulled off his helmet. He glanced up at the elegant condominiums with their black and cream color scheme, the same ones he remembered from three years ago. *What am I doing here?*

Like a magnet to a thick piece of steel, he couldn't resist the pull. He had to see him again.

"You got it so damn bad, Guinness," he groaned, cut the engine, and dismounted.

He hadn't called to even make sure the other guy was

home, but he hadn't actually planned on winding up there. Trekking up the stairs, he played various lines of dialogue inside his head, ones explaining why the hell he'd shown up out of the blue. *I was just passing by and wanted to say hi.* He huffed. Definitely not leading with that. *Hey, I couldn't find my...socks from three years ago?* No. *Um...phone?* Shit. He shook his head. God, that was so lame.

Stopping in front of Max's door, he inhaled deep, hoping like hell the right opening would find its way out of his mouth. Applying his knuckles to the wood, he rapped twice and waited, shuffling back and forth between his feet.

You're getting too attached to this guy.

He squeezed his eyelids tight, doing his best to block out the negative thoughts oozing to the surface like a dark sludge, threatening to swamp him and drag him under. One day at a time—he looped the mantra inside his head, forcing a temporary cap on the rupture.

For right now, he just needed to see him again. He just wanted to maybe hang out for a couple of hours, not forge a lifetime commitment.

The deadbolt clicked, then the door swung open. Max stood in the doorway with his dark curls messy and falling over his forehead. He wore a faded blue T-shirt and a pair of gray shorts, and damn if he wasn't kissable as hell.

Patrick tightened his grip on his helmet. He had to do something because he was about one second away from grabbing the other guy by his shirt, hauling him out into the stairwell, and taking what was his right then and there. But that was the problem, wasn't it? Max wasn't his to keep, right?

"Patrick?" Max's blue eyes widened, brightening. "How did you know I still lived here?" Max shook his head. "I mean, hey there. Wow, come on in." He stepped aside, making room for Patrick to cross the threshold.

Inside, Patrick surveyed the open floor plan. Everything

looked exactly how he remembered it: polished tile floors, granite countertops, and chandeliers. Way beyond his current pay grade. He swallowed hard, pushing past the constriction building in his throat.

Max brushed past him, jostling him back into their conversation. "I recognized the address on your invoice from the other day at the shop." Patrick stepped down into the living space.

"Oh, right." Max nodded. "That makes sense." He headed toward the kitchen. "You want some coffee or something?"

"Nah, I'm good," he said, alternating his helmet between his hands.

"Okay." A pop sounded as Max rounded the counter on his way back into the living room, and he took a swig from a can of Coke. "What's going on, big guy?" Max grinned.

"I was just kind of passing by and thought I'd say hi." Patrick groaned inside his head. Real smooth dude.

The worst line ever.

Of all the excuses, that was the one he defaulted to?

"Actually," Patrick strode over to the sectional sofa and eased down onto the arm, facing Max. He sucked in a deep breath before continuing. "That's not the whole truth."

"It's not?" Max sauntered closer, eyeing him. "Then why are you here, PG?"

"Because no matter how hard I fought it after I got home, I couldn't stay there. The next thing I knew, I was on my bike and steering toward your condo."

Max stepped in front of him, and his palms landed on Patrick's chest. His warmth seared through his shirt, easing him. Damn near melting him.

"I needed to see you," he whispered.

"I like the sound of that." He tugged on the front of Patrick's T-shirt, and Patrick leaned in, gliding his lips over Max's. "I'm glad you're here," he murmured before pulling back. "You don't have to work today?"

"Nope." Patrick blinked at the abrupt change in subject. "Tommie's covering the shop this weekend. Why?"

"Because how about you and I get out of here?" Max strode around the sofa, and Patrick followed.

"What did you have in mind?"

"My family has a place on the lake, and there's nobody up there this weekend. We could grab some food and drinks, ride up there, and spend the afternoon hanging out by the water." He smiled.

It sounded really nice, but he couldn't help wondering… "Your folks would be okay with you taking me up there?"

"Why wouldn't they?" Max's expression twisted with confusion.

"They haven't met me, for one. And I've never thought to ask, but do they even know you're gay?" Patrick cocked an eyebrow. "I'm thinking that would make a big difference to them if you were taking a guy 'friend' up there for a visit."

"Yes, for your information, they know I'm gay. My dad just doesn't want me flaunting it in his face. He'd rather not have to acknowledge it." He shrugged, as if it were perfectly fine that his dad treated him as if he were ashamed of his son.

What a bastard.

"But I do have a key and can use the place anytime I want," Max went on to say. "It's not like we're going up there for a rave or to trash the place. You're my *friend*, and I'm saying you're welcome there."

The nerd was damn convincing when he wanted to be. Perhaps law school was a good choice for Blue Eyes. Patrick smirked. "Let's do this, then."

"Excellent." Max lifted his brows, his eyes gleaming with victory. "I'll change, and we'll hit the road."

About an hour later, Max turned his BMW onto the graveled, circular drive of the Segretis' lake home. The ride up there would have been fun on his motorcycle, but Max didn't own a helmet, so they'd chosen to take Max's car.

Max parked in front of the large cabin and cut the engine. "This is it," he said, glancing in Patrick's direction.

"It's big." He probably should have thought of something more flattering to say about the massive two-story home with its sweeping country front porch supported by giant chiseled logs. But it was accurate.

"Yeah, that's my dad's motto," Max said. "Go big or go home."

They climbed out of the car and grabbed the bags from the back seat. On the way to the lake they'd stopped and picked up a few things to eat, along with some beer and soda.

"The pontoon should be gassed up if you want to go out on the lake," Max said.

"Whatever you think." Patrick followed Max up the steps.

Max unlocked the double front door and proceeded inside. Patrick crossed the threshold, the scent of fresh cedar assaulting his nostrils. The place seemed even larger inside than out. His gaze followed a curved staircase, made of wood and black wrought iron, upward. The ceiling was open all the way to the roof, where two skylights provided access for natural light to flood both levels.

"Come on into the kitchen," Max called out, and Patrick followed the sound of his voice to the rear of the house. The back of the home was almost entirely floor-to-ceiling windows that took advantage of the view of open water as well as a clear blue swimming pool just outside the sliding doors. "Make yourself at home." Max handed him a cold bottle of Bud.

Sliding onto one of the padded stools at the stone bar, Patrick brought the beer up to his lips and took a hard pull. It had been a long time since he'd been inside of a home this loaded. Not since the days before he'd botched up his knee and lost his deal with the Packers.

Though, after being forced to say good-bye not only to his career but to his father, too, all within a two-year span, he was learning there was a hell of lot more to life than football or money.

He didn't begrudge the Segretis their wealth. Not really. There was a time, though, right after he'd drained his bank account of nearly every dollar he'd had left to pay his dad's medical bills and the shop's debt, that he would have. It was a slow process, but he was making peace with his new status in life. However, his brother, it seemed, was still struggling with the sudden loss of their dad and the promise of a new lifestyle Patrick would have been able to give them.

He couldn't help but wonder, though, how deep the vein of resentment would run in Max's dad once he learned Patrick, a broke grease monkey, was in Max's life.

"Everything okay?" Max leaned onto the counter in front of him.

"Yeah." He nodded. "Sure."

"Liar." Max glared at him.

"Nah, man." Patrick shrugged. "I'm good. I was thinking—"

"Stop thinking." He smacked the granite with his palm. "That's your problem. We're supposed to be up here to relax. Have a good time." Max groaned. "I can't believe I just said that. My friend Abbie has been basically yelling those words at me for years." Max rounded the bar toward him. "This afternoon, no one else in the world exists except for you and me."

"I like that idea, Blue Eyes." Patrick lowered his beer onto the stone and cupped Max's ass with his palm, dragging him closer. "So what do you think we should do with all this alone time?" He curled his lip, letting Max know precisely what he'd like to do.

Max leaned in and the blunt edges of his teeth scrapped Patrick's ear lobe. "Nothing I'd like better," he breathed. "But…"

"But?" Patrick pulled away and eyed him.

"We have a pool and a boat at our disposal." Max smiled. "Let's take advantage of having all this to ourselves."

Patrick groaned. "That's what I'm trying to do, if you'd let me."

Chuckling, Max shook his head. "Is sex the only thing you think about?"

"Nope," Patrick said. "I happen to think about football and cars, too, sometimes."

"Oh, right." Max laughed.

Patrick grabbed Max by the nape, drawing him back in, stopping only when his mouth was next to his. "But when you're around…" Patrick sucked in a harsh breath through his teeth. "Fucking you is all that's on my damn mind." He licked the full curve of Max's lower lip before tugging the sensitive flesh in for a nibble.

"Damn, PG." Max panted. "You're killing me. You make it hard for me to keep my head on straight."

"That's the idea, baby."

"Haven't you ever heard the word 'anticipation'?"

He huffed. "Anticipation, huh?"

"Yes. You know, how it's supposed to make things that much sweeter." Max backed away, grinning.

Patrick slid from his seat, straightening to his full height. "Damn ugly rumor."

"Go for a swim with me." Beckoning him with his finger, Max reversed his step toward the patio door.

"And what? Cool off?" Patrick braced his hands on his hips, challenging him, even though the idea did sound great. But he couldn't help teasing Max. He loved how easily he blushed too much.

"That, and I want to hang out with you for a little while." Max glanced over his shoulder at the pool and its array of red and yellow umbrellas and lounge chairs. "Lie around out there, eat, and talk about nothing."

"I didn't bring any trunks," Patrick said. Ending up at the lake with Max had been the last thing he'd expected to happen that day.

"Not a problem. My mom keeps a bunch here in case a guest wants to go for a swim."

"All right." Patrick shook his head. He knew when he'd been beaten. "Let's do this."

A couple of hours later, Patrick lay sprawled on one of the lounge chairs, drinking up the late afternoon sun and listening to the distant buzz of boats motoring across the lake. He had to admit, Max had been right. This was exactly what he needed. The water had felt great, and the stress from the last few weeks felt miles away.

"Having a good time?"

Patrick glanced left. Max lay prone on his lounge chair, looking his way and sporting a big grin. "Yeah, I am. It's so damn peaceful here."

"I like to come up here, especially when I can have the place to myself." He flipped, shoved his sunglasses on, and rested his head on his hands. "How's your brother doing?"

"Pretty good, actually." Patrick filled Max in on the new job situation.

"That's really great."

"It sounds crazy, being as I'm not that much older than Liam is, but I've kind of felt at a loss on to how to help him. I mean, I miss our dad, too. It killed me when he died. But I think for Liam…" Patrick scrubbed his palm over his lower jaw and mouth. "Losing Dad really messed him up, more than I realized."

"You'd been out of the house, living on your own for a

while before your dad passed," Max said. "Liam was still a kid, and with you gone, I imagine your dad was his whole world."

Shaking his head, Patrick stared at Max. "You're right." He sighed. "I'm just hoping he's turning a corner and beginning to feel better."

"He's got you for a big brother," Max said. "I have every confidence the kid's going to be fine."

"Glad you think so." Patrick grunted.

Max climbed from his bright blue cushioned lounge and onto Patrick's. "I do," he said, and straddled Patrick's hips. The sun's rays glistened on the beads of water still clinging to his shoulders after his swim. He leaned forward, bracing his hands on either side of Patrick's head. "You're a very good influence, sir."

Grabbing Max by his upper arms, Patrick tossed him on his side and slung a leg over. "When it comes to you, though, I prefer to think that I'm a very bad influence." He rocked his hips into Max, pressing his growing erection into his lover to nail the point.

"That you are." Max's smile quirked, and he snaked an arm around Patrick's neck. "But I like it." He skated his lips over Patrick's. "I like you," he whispered. "A lot."

"That's good to know," Patrick said. "Since I like you, too." He deepened the kiss, enjoying the sweet taste the soda had left behind on Max's tongue. Back and forth, he thrust into his mouth, playing, stroking. Their tongues dueled, dancing to the erotic vibe beating between them like a drum. "Damn," Patrick breathed.

"Hell, yeah." Max cupped Patrick's face, his thumb dipping down, toying with the corner of his mouth. "I'm curious about something."

"What's that?"

"Proclivity."

"What about it?" Patrick leaned back.

"Do you like to go there often?" Max dropped his hand to Patrick's arm, stroking him as if he were attempting to soothe an animal about to bolt.

"If I do?" he asked. He knew what Max was getting at. He was dancing around the question of whether Patrick was screwing anyone else. Were they exclusive?

"If you do, then I'd want you to take me with you," Max said, his tone calm, matter-of-fact.

The idea of Max walking through those doors again, sitting there as the other members watched him, wanted him, wondered if Patrick planned on sharing his sexy nerd… His blood sizzled and his stomach roiled at the thought.

Hell, no.

"Proclivity was a place I started going to right before my NFL contract ended," he began. "Then after our dad died, and I had to take on the responsibility of my little brother, I needed that refuge. The anonymity. A place where I could let go and then leave it there when I went home."

"I get it," Max said, his voice soft.

"I don't know where this is heading." Patrick lifted the other guy's chin with his thumb and forefinger. "Where we're going… But for now, I do know you're all I need." He leaned back in, allowing his lips and tongue to roam Max's lips. "And I don't share," Patrick rumbled.

Chapter Thirteen

Max was dreaming.

That was the only explanation for how awesome the last few weeks had been. Except he'd pinched himself at least a half dozen times, and nothing happened. He'd been wide-ass awake.

He and Patrick had been spending every possible moment together, whenever they both could get away in the evenings or on the weekends. And Max had never been happier. He grinned, remembering how they'd said good-bye to each other on Sunday night—for a half hour.

Everything was great.

A ghost of a shiver raced over him, and his smile faltered. So why did it feel like he was waiting for the proverbial shoe to drop, to stomp all over the best thing that had ever happened to him? *Oh, yeah.* Because his family had yet to meet Patrick.

Abbie reached around him for the break room's coffee pot. "Have you asked Mr. Football Star to go with you to the Our Legacy event?"

"No," he said, tossing his stirrer in the trash. He grabbed

his cup and settled onto one of the plastic chairs at the table. Abbie was the only person he'd told about Patrick. She'd been thrilled to find out that they were together, and so far she'd done a great job at keeping the news to herself.

"The event is in like three days, right?" She snagged the seat next to him. "He's going to need time to get a tux, you know." She grabbed his arm. "Can you imagine how good he's going to look in that thing?" Her lashes fluttered. "I must see pictures." She gasped. "Better yet, please tell me I can come over and help you dress so I'm there when he arrives to pick you up."

"One…" He held up his index finger. "I never said I was taking anyone to the event. And two…" He added another digit. "Who said *he* would be the one picking *me* up?"

"First, of course you're taking Patrick. Second, because… *Hello*?" She blinked. "I have to see him in his tux!"

Max burst into laughter. "What would I do without you, girl? You never fail to make my day."

"It's a good thing you'll never have to find out." She clasped his hand. "Friends forever, right?"

"Forever."

"So, have you mentioned that you're dating Patrick Guinness to your mom or dad yet?" Abbie sipped from her cup.

"What?" He gulped to keep from spewing his coffee. "No. You know my father isn't ready to deal with me having a steady partner."

"No time like the present to start the process," she said.

One of the other paralegals entered the room, and Max clamped his mouth shut on his response.

"Hi, Abbie." The tall brunette glanced at him. "Max," she said.

"Hey, Yolanda," they replied in unison. Abbie plucked a banana from the fruit bowl in the center of the table and slowly began to peel the yellow layers away.

She reached into the fridge and pulled out a canned weight-loss shake. "I'm never going to last on this crap," she said. "It's an hour before lunch, but I'm already about to chew my tongue for something to eat." She growled, popped the top on her drink, and headed back toward the hall.

"You can do this, Yolanda!" Abbie called out as she left the room.

"Getting back to what you were saying," Max said the moment the other woman disappeared. "You're insinuating that I should take Patrick to the Foundation's event as a sort of icebreaker with my father?"

"Is that what I'm saying?" Her perfectly arched brows lifted.

"That's exactly what you're getting at." Max sat back in his chair, his chest suddenly tighter than it had been five minutes ago. He breathed deep, trying to loosen the anxiety-laden constriction. "That would be more like using a sledgehammer to break the ice rather than a pick."

"Maybe it would be easier on him if he heard about you and Patrick being together at the event without having to be there to witness it. Then, after learning how well you represented the firm there, he would warm up to the idea. Hell, maybe he'd even come to realize that this is the twenty-first century and his son being gay isn't going to ruin the firm's or his family's precious image?"

"It's a beautiful dream, my dear friend," Max said on a long sigh.

Abbie straightened and squared her shoulders. "It could happen, oh ye of little faith!"

"I'll think about it," he said, staring at his cup.

"I just want you to be happy, and I think that, for the first time, you've found someone who does that for you." She reached over and patted the back of his hand. "Don't let the fear of your father's backlash cause you to lose him, love. I know that's easier said than done, coming from someone who doesn't have to face him. But dammit, Max, it frustrates me to no end how the old man dominates your life."

"I know." He swallowed hard, forcing the knot of rising apprehension back down his throat. "And you're right. I'm a grown man, and at some point he and I are going to have to face this. I can't live my life keeping the gender of whom I date out of the public eye for his comfort. It wasn't that big of a deal while I was in college or grad school…mainly because I never had time to date, and I wasn't around him." He exhaled. "But things have changed now. I'm on track to be a full-time attorney here."

"And you're in love," she added.

"And I'm in love," he repeated, before realizing exactly what he'd said. "Wait? Whoa." He sat forward. "I didn't mean—"

"Yes, you did." A smug grin spread on her face. "Max is in love," she whispered in a singsong voice.

"Stop it!" His heart raced at hearing the words out loud. "That slipped out only because I was repeating what you were saying. I don't know that yet."

"You know what they say about those who protest too much." Abbie stood with her cup in hand and walked to the sink.

Was that really some kind of subconscious slip—his head trying to clue his heart in on what was going down?

No. He shook himself. It was too soon. He wasn't the kind of guy who fell in love at the drop of hat, or just because of great sex. Although what he and Patrick had went way beyond "great sex." It was mind-altering, off-the-charts, melt-the-sheets kind of sex.

"That may be what 'they' say, but what I'm telling you is to leave it alone. We haven't been seeing each other for long enough yet for either one of us."

"What does time have to do with anything when it comes to the heart?" She returned to the table and slung an arm over his shoulders. "The heart knows when it's met its soul mate."

Soul mate? Panic tightened the band another notch around his rib cage. "And you know this because of all the success you've had in your love life?"

She pulled away. "Low blow."

"I'm sorry. That was rude." Damn, he shouldn't have said that. "I know you're only trying to be a good friend, and I appreciate your support. More than you'll ever know."

She curled her fingers around the back of a chair, her bubbly persona muted. "I wasn't trying to piss you off. But you know finding love, a real connection with someone, doesn't happen that often in life. Don't blow it, Max." Abbie strolled toward the door. "I've got to get back to work," she added on her way out.

The day moved forward at the speed of a slug. Normally he enjoyed his work, the law, but today he just needed to get away from the firm and see Patrick again.

Abbie's declaration had gotten under his skin.

Probably because she was right.

If he didn't start walking the walk, and proving to Patrick that the fact they came from two different worlds wasn't a big deal, he would eventually lose him.

Five o'clock finally rolled around, and unlike his typical habit, he beat everyone else to their car. Inside the protection of his BMW, he dialed Patrick on his cell and made plans for them to meet for dinner at Bella's.

That was the easy part.

Convincing the big guy to attend a black tie event with him… Yeah, that was going to take a whole lot of finesse. Plus a bottle or two of wine.

...

A couple of hours and a half bottle of wine later, Max pushed his lasagna around with his fork, waiting for the right thing to say—the right opening to present itself. He didn't have to look up to know Patrick studied him. The heat of his gaze burned into him.

"Are you ready to talk about why we're having dinner tonight?" Patrick topped off their glasses with more Chianti.

Damn, he was too perceptive. Max lifted his head. "What are you talking about? Do I need a reason to ask you to dinner?"

"Nope," he said. "Not really. I can just tell something has been eating away at you all evening. So why don't you go ahead and spill it."

Lowering his fork onto his napkin, Max inhaled deep. "I wanted to see you tonight. That's the truth. But I'll admit, there's more to it."

"I knew it." Patrick wrapped his fingers around his glass and brought it to his lips.

"How would you feel about being my plus one this Saturday?" There. He'd done it. His stomach flipped, and he snagged his own wineglass, needing a gulp.

"Your plus one?" Patrick's brow lifted, and he set his glass back on the table. "Is this a wedding or something?"

Max nodded. "Or something."

"Meaning?"

"My parents attend an event every year for the Our Legacy Foundation. It's an educational fund for underprivileged children. The event is this Saturday, and my father has asked me to go in their place this year." Max pushed his plate aside and reached over to cover Patrick's hand with his own. "I'd love for you to be my date."

"Seriously?" Patrick pulled away and sat back against the

booth. "This sounds like a black tie event involving anyone who's anyone showing up to pull out their checkbooks. Which also means there will be press." His date scowled.

"I know." Max nodded. "And that's a problem, why?"

"It may not be for you," Patrick said, his tone snide. "But you know there's no good reason why I should be there. I don't have the kind of bank account that would warrant me an invite."

"You would be there as my date. That doesn't mean you have to be a donor."

"So what happens when the press asks who I am? You mean to tell me you'd be okay telling everyone you have a mechanic on your arm?" Patrick fisted his glass and downed another mouthful of wine.

"You're also a former Packer. But even if you weren't, I'm not embarrassed that you work on cars." Damn him for thinking that he was! "Your job—your business—provides for you and Liam. And as long as you're happy, that's all that matters to me." Max leaned back against his seat. "I would be thrilled to announce to the whole fucking world that Patrick Guinness is my date. You know why?"

Patrick shot him a glare right before he rested his forearms on the table, closing some of the distance between them. "Why?"

"Because he's the best damn guy I've ever known." Max clasped his fingers around one of Patrick's wrists.

A weak chuckle erupted up from Patrick, and his head lowered. "That's funny…" he said, as he looked up, his hazel gaze finding Max's. "Because I feel the same way about you."

Max's heart swelled, and he had no idea how the thing managed to stay inside his rib cage. "So you're not going to make me go to this thing alone?"

A groan rumbled from Patrick's throat. "Fine." He shook his head. "I can't believe I'm doing this."

Laughing, Max grabbed his wineglass and clinked it against Patrick's stationary one. "Yes! Cheers! This will be great." He took a sip. "Oh! We have to get you a tux."

"I have one stashed away in my closet somewhere. It should still fit okay." He leaned into the table. "You're lucky you're so damn hot and that I have a hard time saying no to you."

"You think I'm hot?" Max eased forward, their lips mere inches apart. The proximity made his pulse race, his breathing reduced to short pants.

"Why don't we head back to your place, and I'll prove it to you."

"Now, that's an offer I can't refuse."

Chapter Fourteen

Thank God Liam had to work tonight.

Patrick pulled his pickup into one of the vacant parking spaces outside of Max's condo, shoved it into park, and cut the engine. Glancing down, he assessed his clothes once more. If his brother had been home, he would have had to lie about why he'd pulled his tux out of retirement.

And he hated lying to Liam.

But the timing had worked out perfectly. His brother had gone into work early and would be staying over at a friend's house for the night. Not having to explain his plans was a hell of lot easier than a blatant lie.

Patrick exited his truck and headed up the stairs to Max's condo. The best part about the situation was he was handling things the way his brother wanted. Liam told him he didn't want to know the details about who he'd been seeing. The less the kid knew about Max and how often they were together, the better. For everyone.

At the top of the landing, he rapped on Max's door. He still couldn't believe he'd allowed himself to get sucked into

a black-tie event. However, a small part of him knew that
when and if Max ever needed him, he'd be there. No matter
what. Yet, the feeling was alien to his psyche. It was a foreign
sensation that he'd gotten this close to a man. So close that
he'd show up in a damn monkey suit just because Max said he
wanted him there.

Truth be told, he kind of liked it.

The deadbolt clicked, and then the door swung open. A
familiar tall brunette with long, reddish-brown curls stood in
the doorway, wearing a pair of shredded cutoff jeans, short
boots, and a fitted T-shirt.

"Patrick." She grinned, hanging on to the door. "You
haven't changed one bit since your Gamecock days," she
drawled and closed the door behind him.

Patrick stepped down into the living space. "Well, I don't
know about that."

"Oh, I do." She joined him in the room and stuck out
her hand. "I'm Abbie Donovan. We met at the firm the other
day." He slid his palm into hers for a brief shake. "Max and I
have been friends since USC. Best friends," she added.

Message received, loud and clear. She was protective of
her friends. He respected that.

"A true friend is hard to come by," he said. "I'm glad Max
has you in his corner."

"They definitely are, and he does." She nodded. "Likewise,
I know he's got my back, too. He's proved it more than once."

"Great. You're here." Max's voice came from behind him.
"I see you two are already getting to know one another."

Patrick pivoted on his heel.

And froze.

Damn...the guy was created to wear a tux. He wore a
black bow tie, white shirt with a tiny black-button detail, and
a black jacket, exactly as Patrick did. But somehow he made
the elegant attire look even more refined.

"Wow," Max said, raking him from head to toe with his gaze. "You were so right, Abbie."

"Yes, I was," Abbie drawled with an appreciative tone.

"Right about what?" Patrick crossed his arms, suddenly feeling the one on the outside of an inside joke.

"You look amazing in your tux."

"Oh…" Patrick gave himself another quick once-over. "Thanks. But look who's talking." Patrick perused his date once more from head to toe. "Fantastic," he said.

"Thank you." Max beamed. "You ready to do this?"

"Sure." Patrick nodded. "As ready as I'll ever be."

Max grabbed his keys and wallet from the counter, and Patrick followed him toward the exit.

"Wait!" Abbie called out, and Max drew to a halt at the door. "You have to get a picture of this. There is way too much hotness in this room right now to not commemorate the moment."

"Really, Abbie?" Max groaned, but hooked his arm in Patrick's.

"God, yes," she said. "Someone hand over their phone."

Abbie was pushy, but in an adorable kind of way. He could see why Max liked her. Patrick tugged his phone out of his pants pocket. "Here, use mine." He handed it to her. "I'll send it to you," he told Max.

"Okay, here we go." Abbie held the phone up. "Show me some teeth, boys." She grinned, and it was infectious. Smiling, Patrick pressed a little closer to Max's shoulder, and Abbie snapped the picture. She glanced down at the screen. "Perfect," she said. "I love it!" Looking up, she handed the phone back to Patrick. "Once you get that shot, you better send it to me, Max." She propped her hands on her hips.

"I promise." Max chuckled. "All right." He released his hold on Patrick and grabbed the door, pulling it open. "We have to get out of here, or we're going to be late." He headed out into the corridor, and Patrick followed.

"Have a blast, you two," Abbie called out, standing in the doorway.

"Thanks," Max yelled over his shoulder, already trekking down the stairs. "See you Monday!"

The drive into downtown Columbia took about twenty minutes. Since technically Patrick was Max's date, they rode in Max's BMW. Not to mention that pulling up to the valet and exiting Patrick's pickup in tuxedos would look a little odd.

"Have I told you lately how glad I am that you're with me tonight?" Max rolled under the hotel's covered drive and into the valet parking zone.

"Not in the last ten minutes." Patrick smirked.

Patrick's door opened before Max could respond. "Good evening, sir," the valet said.

"Thanks," Patrick said, and stepped from the Beamer. Max joined him in front the hotel's revolving door as the attendant drove off.

Inside, Patrick followed alongside his date to the establishment's grand ballroom. Instrumental music wafted through the open double doors as they neared a gathering of attendees dressed in glittery evening gowns.

"Well, look who we have here," one of the women, with her dark hair stacked impossibly high on her head, exclaimed. "Maximo's son!" She zeroed in on Max, giving him a Hollywood kiss to each cheek. "I haven't seen you since you were a teenager." Beehive gripped his arms and stepped back, giving him a once-over. "My, what a good-looking man you've become." She smiled. "Is your father here with you tonight?"

"No, ma'am," Max said. "I'm representing the firm this evening."

"Oh, how nice." She glanced behind him. "And where is your lovely date?"

"He's right here." Max placed a palm to the center of

Patrick's back.

Damn, now that was bold. Right off the bat without hesitation. His nerd had guts, especially when it came to being out and proud in the Bible belt.

She blinked, as if her mind needed a moment to grasp the concept. "Oh, I don't believe we've met," she said, her smile faltering for a moment before she kicked it back into place and held out her hand.

"Madeline Freeman," Max said, "may I introduce Patrick Guinness."

Patrick clasped her hand for a gentle shake. "It's my pleasure," he said.

"You're not what I expected," she said hanging on to Patrick's hand. "But I have to say you have wonderful taste, Max." She glanced at his date and winked.

Well, okay then. That was not what *he* had expected. "Thank you, ma'am," Patrick said, pulling his palm free. "I'm flattered."

"We must have a dance before the night is over," she said.

"Of course. I'd love to," Patrick added.

"Good." She grinned. "I'll see you two inside, then."

Max leaned into him. "Besides her dance, you're all mine."

Cupping Max's jaw, Patrick lifted the other guy's chin. "All yours," he whispered.

In the ballroom, seating was around large, circular tables placed strategically in front of an elevated platform. Camera flashes dotted the scene as he and Max took their places for dinner. Patrick hadn't seen this much media since the draft.

To his relief, the meal went off without drama, and he was actually having a nice time. At the completion of dinner, Max left the table and approached the podium. His speech was eloquent and composed. Hell, Max was damn good up there. Heat welled behind his breastbone, as if someone had cracked open a warm bottle of oil inside his chest. He palmed the area, trying to contain the sensation, to keep it from bubbling over and turning him to mush. Shit! What the hell? He didn't do touchy-feely.

God help him. He couldn't be falling that hard for the guy. Things were still too damn complicated for something that heavy. Hell, he and Liam hadn't even been able to have a normal conversation yet about the fact he was dating Max.

"The Segreti family would like to start off the donations with a check for five hundred thousand dollars," Max said. The figure rang inside Patrick's head as applause filled the large room.

A half of a million dollars? Max's family could drop a half million on a charity without blinking an eye. And here he sat wondering how they were going to manage to pay the bills at the shop. Not to mention paying back the loan he'd had to take out for Liam's legal fees. His stomach twisted at the thought. He and Max were so far from the same page in life.

The next instant, he was on his feet heading toward the door, except he barely remembered leaving the table. He had to get some air. He was suffocating, his chest too tight.

Patrick punched the lock-bar on the door and marched out. On the other side, he rested his back against the wall. What the fuck was he doing there? How was a relationship with Max ever going to last? Inevitably, Max would realize that he needed something—someone—more in his life. Someone he had more in common with than he did with a guy who operated a suspension repair shop. And Patrick would end up paying the price for trying to make this fantasy work. He stared down at his monkey suit and barked out a sick laugh.

The door clanked open beside him. "There you are."

Max.

"I was wondering where you ran off to. Is everything okay?"

"Yeah. Sure." He nodded and swallowed hard, forcing the knot back down his throat. "I just needed some air. It got kind of stuffy in there."

"Stuffy is the right word for it." Max chuckled. "I promise we don't have to hang out much longer. But unfortunately I have to schmooze for a few more minutes."

"No problem." Patrick scrubbed a hand over his face. "I understand."

"You ready to head back in?" Max straightened and adjusted his suit.

"Right behind you." Patrick followed Max back inside, and the noise of the crowd and the music swamped him the moment the doors opened. With the dinner over, the attendees were mingling and taking to the dance floor.

"Mr. Segreti," a man called out as he rushed them both. "Brad Hutto, with the Palmetto Daily." He glanced in Patrick's direction. "I was hoping you'd introduce our readers to your date tonight."

Patrick internally groaned. Guess he'd been an idiot to hope they'd dodged that bullet.

"Absolutely," Max said, placing a palm to Patrick's back. "This is Patrick Guinness."

"Guinness?" The reporter cocked his head. "Patrick Guinness, the USC running back who went pro about three years ago?"

He nodded. "That would be me," Patrick said.

"Wow, man." Brad shook his head. "I was so sorry to hear about your knee. That totally sucked."

"Totally." Patrick painted on a tolerant smile.

"So what are you doing now?" The guy edged closer. "Are you here in the Columbia area?"

Patrick glanced Max's way. This was his night, his charity, not the Patrick Guinness story. Besides, no way in hell did he want his story casting a shadow on what Max had done this evening to help underprivileged kids.

"Patrick owns and manages his late father's business on the northeast side of town," Max interjected.

Shit! Patrick closed his eyes briefly and sucked in a stabilizing breath.

"You've probably heard of it—Guinness Tire and Wheel Alignment. His father began the business years ago, and now Patrick is carrying on his legacy."

Damn, the way Max spun his career, one would have thought he had a seat on the county council instead of managing a few guys in a garage.

Perhaps he had a point, though, about his father's legacy. Wasn't that what he was doing by working his ass off to keep the shop afloat? Making sure that the men his father had hired still had a job and could pay their mortgage? He'd lost his dream of the NFL. But hell…maybe this is where he was supposed to be? And maybe—just maybe—his dad would still be proud of him.

"Yes, I have," Brad said. "I took my van there last year. I'm very sorry for your loss, Mr. Guinness," he added.

"Thank you." Patrick shoved his hands in his pockets.

"You're welcome. And thank you both for taking the time to answer a few questions for me tonight." He headed off into the crowd.

Patrick opened his mouth, ready to thank Max for diving in and offering a response to the reporter, when Mrs. Freeman appeared, a smile parting her red-painted lips.

"There you are, Mr. Guinness," she exclaimed. "I thought for a moment you'd left before I'd gotten my dance with you."

"Now, how could I ever think of leaving before I had the opportunity to spin a lovely lady like yourself around the dance floor?" Patrick met her smile with one of his own and extended his arm. "Would you do me the honor of dancing with me, Mrs. Freeman?"

"I would love to." Her cheeks reddened, and she took his arm.

"You two enjoy yourselves out there," Max called out as they made their way onto the dance floor.

Another hour had passed before Patrick and Max finally climbed into the car.

"Would you have ever believed that Madeline Freeman was capable of moves like that?" Max laughed, pulling the Beamer into the flow of traffic.

"Never. And my aching knee can attest to that fact." Patrick couldn't believe it, but damn, he'd actually ended up having fun. Max had seemed completely at ease with him—with the whole night. Maybe he'd been overreacting about their situation?

Who, me? Overreact?

Never!

Only when it came to football, commitments, money, and his brother. He chuckled to himself.

"Oh, shit," Max said, drawing him back into the conversation. "It didn't occur to me that dancing with her might be a problem for your knee."

"It's okay. Don't worry about it." Patrick massaged to his kneecap. "As long as it's not something I'm trying to do every weekend, I'm all good."

"Oh, okay." Max adjusted the temp on the AC. "I'm glad dancing didn't make things worse."

"Nah. I'll ice it if it doesn't calm down, and it'll be fine." Easing back against the seat, he studied the elegant profile of his date. The perfectly straight line of his nose. The sexy-ass dimple at the corner of his mouth. And speaking of that mouth… His cock twitched. Damn, he had gorgeous lips. "You know," he began, "I never did get to see your moves out there on the floor."

"My moves?" Max glanced at him and laughed. "What

makes you think I have any moves?"

"Oh, trust me." He repositioned himself. "I know you've got moves."

"Are we still talking about dancing?" The man's fuck-me dimple deepened at the corner of his mouth, sending all the blood from Patrick's brain straight to his cock. Hell no, he wasn't talking about dancing.

"Liam's not going to be home tonight," Patrick said, his growing arousal deepening the timbre of his voice. "We could go back to my house. If you wouldn't mind taking me to get my truck from your place in the morning?"

Max glanced over at Patrick for a moment, then back to road. "This night just keeps getting better." He grinned. "First, there was you in a tux in my living room. And I have to say, dayuuum, PG. Then you on the dance floor doing some kind of move with Mrs. Freeman that could only be described as 'the bump.'" He shook his head. "How much of a good time can one gay man handle in one evening?"

Patrick palmed Max's nape, lightly tugging on his hair. "Kiss my ass, Segreti."

"When and where, big guy?" Max whispered. "When and where?"

"Take me home and I'll tell you, Blue Eyes." Patrick released his grip on Max's hair and eased back into his seat, facing forward. Inhaling deep, he curled his fist around the leather-wrapped bar to the door. If he didn't do something, he would be jerking the steering wheel, sending the car onto the shoulder of the road, and showing the sexy nerd what a real good time was all about. His erection bucked in approval. Patience had never been his virtue.

But in the interest of safety, and not being arrested for public indecency, he'd have to make an effort.

"There's been no one else but you since that first night," Patrick found himself saying, the words tumbling from his mouth like a broken faucet. Since they had time to kill, there was no time like the present to get it all out there.

Focusing on the yellow lines in the road, he kept going. "Not since that evening I followed you into the men's room at the pub have I been with anyone else." He swallowed hard and pushed forward with the info he needed to share. "I went to our family doc and got tested. Not because I've ever been careless, but because I owed it to you to make sure I was clean." He risked a glance in Max's direction, the silence too painful to bear any longer. Max stared straight ahead through the windshield, his expression unreadable.

"Are you okay?" Max asked, his question barely above a whisper.

"Yeah." Patrick rubbed an open palm on his thigh. "Everything came back good."

"Great," Max said, flexing his fingers around the steering wheel. "I'm glad you brought it up, because I've been wanting to talk to you about the same thing, but there never seemed to be the right time. I haven't been with anyone other than you since I've been back from law school. But before I left to come home, I got tested at the clinic there. I'm good. All my tests were negative."

"That's good." Patrick exhaled and smoothed a palm over his mouth and jaw. "Really good news."

Max must have sensed the tenuous hold of Patrick's control, because he had them home in record time.

At the door, Patrick shoved the key in the deadbolt, twisted his wrist, and flung the door open for Max to enter. He brushed past him, and Patrick kicked the door shut, flipping the switch near the entrance to turn on a lamp on the other side of the room. That was about the only warning he gave to Max before he had his lover's back pressed against the wall, his hands above his head with his wrists clamped tight within his grip.

He slammed his mouth onto Max's, too eager to wait for an invitation, or even permission. He needed him now, like this, Max's body writhing against his. Patrick sank his teeth into the tender flesh of Max's lower lip. Max grunted and his hips bucked, shoving his erection against Patrick's.

"You like that, baby?" Patrick ground his cock into the hard feel of Max's.

"Yes," Max whispered.

"You like it when I'm control?"

"You know I do."

Releasing Max's wrists, Patrick glided his palms down along his arms, enjoying the smooth, silky feel of the tuxedo's fabric beneath his fingertips. He tucked his fingers beneath Max's jacket and helped him to shrug it off and drop it to the floor. "Did I tell you how much I like the way you look in your tux?"

"I don't mind hearing it again."

Patrick worked open the button on Max's trousers and proceeded to tug on the zipper. "Come with me."

He backed away, and Max followed. At the large leather chair in the den, Patrick stopped. "Sit," he ordered.

Max lowered himself onto the cushion, his trousers open at the waist. Leaning in, Patrick seized one end of Max's bow tie and pulled, loosening it from around his neck. "You were made to wear fine clothes like this, Blue Eyes."

He trailed his fingers lower until he was back where he'd left off: at the fly to Max's trousers. Pushing the fabric aside, Patrick reached in, nudging open the other guy's briefs, and wrapped his fingers around Max's cock. Max hissed, and his hips rocked on the seat. Patrick pulled Max's hard-on free and straightened, drinking in the sight of his lover still dressed in his tux, with his erection, thick and glistening, jutting out from between the folds of his trousers. "Son of a bitch," he bit out.

At that moment he didn't give a shit about the rest of

the world—what anyone else thought. They could all fuck themselves. Because all he'd ever wanted in his life was right there, sitting in front of him.

"Touch yourself," Patrick demanded.

Max complied, fisting his cock. He pulled on his shaft, his eyelids shuttering.

"Does that feel good, baby?" Patrick reversed his step until the backs of his legs bumped the chair facing Max's.

The pink tip of his lover's tongue appeared, and he licked his lower lip. "Yes," he breathed.

"Good." Patrick unzipped his pants and loosened his own necktie before lowering himself onto the seat. "Look at me, Blue Eyes," Patrick ordered, palming his cock and tugging it free. Max lifted his eyelids.

"Holy fuck," his lover muttered.

"Do you like what you see?"

"Shit." Max pulled on his shaft.

"Is that a yes?" Patrick mimicked the move of his lover's hand.

"Yes."

"Does it turn you on, watching me stroke my dick, knowing that it's you who's on my mind? It's you that's got me like this, my cock so fucking hard it hurts."

Max groaned and released the hold on his erection. "Dammit, PG."

"No," Patrick scolded. "You don't stop until I say you can."

"I'll come if you keep talking to me like that, looking at me like that," Max said, but he did as he was told, wrapping his fingers back around his erection.

"No. You won't." Patrick glided his fingertips over the backside of his own shaft, teasing, testing the depths of his control over his orgasm. Such a fucking rush. "Not until I say you can."

A grunt was Max's only response, but he kept his hand moving up and down his cock, circling just beneath the rim.

"Show me what feels good, baby. Watching you, knowing that every stroke is taking you so close to the edge, is driving me so fucking crazy."

"Christ…Patrick." He squeezed his eyes shut. "Need to… hurts." He groaned, his hips bucking into his fist.

"Open your eyes," Patrick commanded, and Max blinked as if his vision had blurred. "Look at me." Max's gaze roamed, then zeroed in on him. "You're mine, Max Segreti," Patrick growled and stood. "Your next orgasm is mine. When you come for me, baby, I plan to drink you dry."

"For you," Max whispered, nodding. In the soft glow of the lamp, sweat glistened on his forehead. "I want to come for you. Oh, fuck." He gritted his teeth. "Now. Please let me come."

Patrick stroked his cock, pre-cum slickening his fingers. "You have no idea how much control it's taking for me not to turn you over and fuck you right now. To let your ass pull my cock inside." Patrick's balls tightened, threatening to shoot his load at the thought. Hissing, he clamped down on his shaft with his fist. "You have the tightest ass, baby."

"Patrick!" Max grunted. "I can't…" His head thrashed, and cum spurted from the head of his cock.

"Hang on, baby." Patrick dropped to his knees between Max's legs.

"Can't stop!"

"It's okay. I got you." Wrapping his fingers over Max's erection, Patrick guided his lover's erupting shaft to his mouth. Max groaned, releasing his grip, and Patrick took his cock to the back of his throat. He convulsively swallowed, wanting it all. All of him. Allowing a guy to shoot off in his mouth had never been something he enjoyed. In fact, he usually did everything he could to avoid the act. But with Max, watching him come, tasting him in the process, was quickly becoming an all-time favorite.

Patrick lifted his head, dragging his tongue up the backside of Max's cock until he'd savored the final drops of cum from his lover's slit. A loud groan sounded, and Max's hips bucked.

"That was…damn. I can't even think," Max breathed, his eyes hooded.

Rising up, Patrick crawled over the chair, boxing the other man in with his arms. "You're spectacular, baby," he said and clutched his face, forcing Max to look up. "Everything about you." He glided his mouth over Max's for a quick taste and lick. "But I have to fuck you now, or I'm going to lose my mind."

"God, yes," Max muttered. "Want you."

"I don't have a condom, and I don't want one." Patrick settled his forehead on Max's, despite the fact his heart, his body, screaming for action. But he had to make sure Max understood and was onboard first. "You okay with that?"

"More than okay," he whispered.

Thank God Max wanted it as much as he did, because at that moment, it would have killed him to use one. He was dying to feel him wrapped around his cock. "Turn over," he said.

Max pushed up from the chair, and Patrick eased back, giving him room to maneuver. While he changed positions, Patrick quickly retrieved a tube of lube from his backpack and returned. With his lover on his knees in the chair, Patrick worked Max's pants down over his ass, pushing them to his knees. Fuck, he had the most delicious backside. After placing a dollop of the lube onto his fingertips, he traced a circle around his lover's opening, attempting to relax the puckered ring. Patrick's hand trembled with restraint.

The incessant, driving urge to be inside him had reached the boiling point. And it was all he could do to force himself to give Max a moment to prepare.

Max groaned and pushed back. "Patrick...I'm ready."

His pleas were the final yank, snapping his control. Patrick slid one finger deep.

"Christ! Yes," his lover moaned. "More."

Adding a second finger, Patrick worked his opening. "Good, baby?"

With his free hand, Patrick fisted his own throbbing cock. He hissed at the contact. Pre-cum dripped from the head. Fuck... He was too close to the edge.

"So good," Max muttered, rocking his hips.

He pulled his fingers free and pressed the end of his shaft to Max's entrance. "Can't wait any longer, baby," he groaned.

"Fuck me, PG," Max growled.

Patrick surged forward, sinking his cock balls deep. Max's hot depths gripped him, the pleasure scorching. Max cried out, clenching onto his shaft, destroying him. The earth tilted, and his balls tightened, ready to blow.

"Fuck..." Patrick grasped the sides of the chair, reclaiming his hold on his balance. Too good. Max rocked, pumping Patrick's cock. Cum slammed into the fragile barrier he'd built on his orgasm. "Don't," Patrick bit out, grabbing on to Max. "Too close."

"Got to," Max groaned, pushing against him. "Need you."

Gritting his teeth, Patrick eased his shaft back until only the head remained inside. He'd never fucked without a condom before, and the sensation was more than he'd expected. Better than he'd ever imagined. Especially knowing his first time was with Max. He slammed home.

Someone cried out, the sound familiar.

Was it him? Max? Who the fuck knew? His mind had altered. Sharpened. His only thought, only purpose, was *more*. He needed more of Max.

Over and over, he pounded into Max, his body no longer

his to control. The need for pleasure was his master, driving him faster, harder.

"Patrick!" Max called out. "Fuck…Patrick!"

Cum exploded from Patrick's shaft, staggering him. "Max!" he shouted, falling forward.

His lover groaned, and rhythmic pulses milked Patrick's cock.

"Damn, baby," he muttered, his hips jerking with each pulse, taking him deep. He buried his face against Max's neck, breathing him in. The sweet scent that was uniquely Max flooded his nostrils, reminding him of lazy, hot summer days. Christ, he never wanted to leave.

"Blue Eyes," he whispered, his orgasm subsiding. "I—"

"Holy hell, PG." Max shifted beneath him.

Patrick swallowed hard, blocking the three words that had bubbled up from his heart. What the hell had he almost done? He'd nearly ruined whatever it was they had by allowing his emotions to short-circuit his brain. Stepping back, Patrick pulled free.

Max placed a shaky leg onto the floor. Patrick caged him in, making sure he was steady before moving away. Slowly the other man straightened and faced him.

"Holy hell." Max shook his head.

"You said that already." Patrick smiled.

"It's worth repeating." He draped his arms around Patrick's neck. "You made me come twice, big guy," he drawled.

"Did I, now?" Patrick lifted a brow and pulled the other guy tight against his abdomen. "Sounds like I was doing something right."

"Yes, you were." Max tugged Patrick's head lower. The blunt edges of his teeth scored the outer shell of his ear, sending a shiver over him and into the head of his shaft. His dick flexed, reawakening. "But don't get cocky. The night's not over yet."

"You keep doing that and I'll reintroduce you to cocky." Patrick cupped the other guy's ass, giving it a squeeze. "If we're going to keep points for how often we come, why don't you follow me into the shower, baby, and I'll give you a chance to even the score?"

Max laughed, pulled away, and finished stepping out of his shoes and trousers. "Damn, I never could say no to a challenge." He smirked. "Which way, big guy?"

Chapter Fifteen

Patrick's warm breath tickled Max's ear, and a snore followed on its heels. He grinned, delighting in the sound of his lover and the warmth of his chest pressed against his back. They'd come so far in the past couple of months.

He eased out from under Patrick's arm and swung his legs over the side of the bed. Grabbing his boxer briefs from the pile of clothes they'd dropped by the bed earlier, he pulled them on. When he glanced at Patrick's sleeping profile, his heart throbbed. He cared so damn much for the other man it literally hurt. Patrick had invited him to spend the night, and he'd admitted there'd been no one else since they'd started seeing each other. Max was his only lover.

He should be on cloud nine.

And he would be…if it weren't for the nagging sense of dread plaguing him about the hurdle he'd yet to scale with his family.

Padding into the kitchen, Max targeted the refrigerator. His tongue felt like a desert. He'd worked up a thirst from their earlier activities. His mind wandered back a couple of hours to when he'd joined Patrick in the shower and successfully evened the score between them. He chuckled to himself, recalling the loud crash when Patrick had grabbed for the nearest handhold as he'd begun coming down Max's throat.

At the refrigerator, Max yanked on the door, and a blast of cold air enveloped his naked torso. On a shelf in the back he spotted a few bottles of water and grabbed one of them. He closed the door, cracked open the cap, and started on his return trip to Patrick's room. Movement out the corner of his eye sent a blast of adrenaline into his bloodstream. His pulse stuttered then raced into high gear. Max darted toward where he thought the light switch should be. His bottle hit the floor, spraying water across the linoleum.

But the other guy beat him to the wall.

"This what you're going for," a deep voice said, and light flooded the kitchen.

Max came to a screeching halt, his pulse a thunderous beat in his ears. He squinted in the bright light to make out the face of the intruder.

"Liam?" Relief washed over him. "What the hell? You almost scared the shit out of me."

Patrick's brother stood there with his arms crossed, his expression twisted into an "it figures" look. "Max Segreti." He shook his head. "Of course it's you. You're the only person I could think of who'd have a BMW parked in our driveway in the middle of the night." Scowling, Liam perused him from top to bottom. "Fucking my brother at your place getting boring?"

"That's enough," Patrick bellowed from the hallway, then appeared behind Liam. "You're not going to talk to Max like that."

Liam faced his brother. "Then you should have thought of that before you brought him back here for your sex games."

"You told me you weren't going to be home tonight," Patrick spat.

"Kyle got sick," Liam said. "So I decided to come home."

"Hey, listen," Max said, feeling beyond awkward standing there half naked in front of Patrick's brother. "I should probably go."

"No," Patrick said. "You're my guest, and you shouldn't have to leave because of my brother."

"It's okay. Really." Max started for the bedroom. "I think it'll be best if I just go."

"Why don't you do that," Liam muttered, bringing Max to a halt.

Wow. What had he ever done to him?

"Liam." Patrick surged forward, putting himself in his brother's face. "I swear to God. Open your mouth again, and I'll—"

"You'll what?" Liam cocked his head, taunting him. "You'll hit me?"

A sharp inhale sounded from Patrick. "No. I'm not going to hit you." He backed away, his hands up as if in surrender. "But your actions tonight, the things you said to Max, really hurt me." He shook his head. "I'm so disappointed in you, kid."

The expression on the younger guy's face telegraphed it all: a physical blow couldn't have hurt worse than what Patrick had said.

Patrick looked over at Max. "I'm riding with you. I need to get my truck."

"Oh, yeah. That's right." Max brushed past him. "I'll get dressed and we can head out."

The next few minutes passed in strained silence, even after they'd finally climbed into his car. Max pulled onto the dark street and accelerated in the direction of his condo. For several miles, the yellow lines in the road flicked past in rapid succession, the only sound between them was the hum of the engine. Was this how they were going to end? Were Liam and his issues going to be what pulled the pin on the grenade, blowing up whatever chance they had to be together?

Damn it! He understood that Patrick had a hell of a lot to deal with, but he couldn't take the silence anymore. "Sooo… any idea why Liam hates my guts so much?"

Patrick sighed, as if the burden of their situation was too much to bear. "I knew he wasn't happy about us seeing each other. So to keep things civil at home, I didn't talk about us, and he didn't ask any questions."

"But why?" Max glanced in Patrick's direction. "What's his beef with me? With us?"

"I guess he thinks that I'm an idiot for getting involved with you." Patrick hit the window button, lowering the glass. He closed his eyes and laid his head back, allowing the wind to rush over him.

"Because I come from money?"

"Bingo," Patrick said, never opening his eyes.

Of course. Wasn't money always the issue?

Max twisted his fist over the leather of his steering wheel, working the material until it squeaked under the pressure. He knew that was exactly what Patrick had believed in the beginning, but lately it felt like things had changed. Had he been wrong? *Shit.* The acrid taste of bile hit the back of his throat, but he forced it down.

"How do you feel about that?" he finally managed to ask. "Have you been an idiot?"

He pulled his car into the vacant spot alongside Patrick's truck and killed the engine. The roar of the motor faded, leaving the sound of their breathing to fill the cabin.

Patrick pulled the handle, and the door popped open. "I think my brother needs to worry more about his own life and let me live mine," he said before climbing out the car.

Was that supposed to be a no?

Evasive much, PG?

Max exited the vehicle intent on getting a real answer. But before he could utter another word, Patrick rounded the Beamer's hood and caught Max's arms, holding him in place. "I'm sorry about how things ended tonight," he said, his voice deepening, his tone sincere. "My brother was out of line."

"It's okay," Max found himself saying. "You can't control how he thinks or feels."

"I know. You're right. But you know what's even harder sometimes?" Patrick pulled him closer, not stopping until Max's chest pressed against his.

"Tell me," Max whispered, mesmerized by the intensity in the other man's eyes.

"Controlling your own damn feelings."

Without warning, Patrick's mouth claimed Max's. His hands drove into Max's hair, his fingers snagging the strands, pulling at the roots. But it didn't matter. The sting only enhanced the urgency, the excitement. This wasn't a good night kiss, or even making out. Max grabbed on to the other man's shoulder, determined to hang on. To hang on to Patrick. Then his tongue was inside, slashing, thrusting at Max's, as if somehow his desperation, his need, had pissed him off. Max moaned, accepting whatever Patrick needed to give him.

On a gasp, Patrick pulled back. "I don't know how this is going to work out," he said, his thumb drawing lazy circles at the corner of Max's mouth. "But I want to see where this goes."

"Me, too," Max whispered, his heart pounding. "But what about Liam?"

"I'll try to make Liam understand. Somehow." His hands fell away from Max's head, and Patrick stepped back. "All I know is that I'm not ready to let you go."

"Don't you dare, Patrick Guinness."

He nodded, his mouth a tight line of determination as he rounded the hood of his truck. Seconds later, the engine rumbled to life, and his pickup pulled away, leaving Max on the sidewalk, his world forever changed.

Whatever doubts he'd had left about how he felt about Patrick had been shattered. He was so totally in love with the guy.

• • •

Not picking up his cell to call Patrick the rest of the weekend had been hell. At work on Monday, Max dropped into the task chair in front of his desk and logged into his PC. He wasn't completely surprised to have not heard from Patrick on Sunday after what had gone down with his guy's brother. That was the main reason he'd refrained from calling. If Patrick hadn't made the attempt to contact him, then he and Liam must have needed the uninterrupted time to work things out.

"Oh my God! You cruel, cruel man," Abbie announced, coming in from the back hall, her purse on her shoulder.

"Are you referring to me?" Max hit her with his best innocent look.

Abbie marched past him. "Do you see anyone else in the room?"

Turning in his chair, he followed her movements. "What did I do to you?"

"Seriously, Max." She dropped her bag, faced him, and cocked her hip. "Were you so busy that you couldn't pick up your phone and let a friend know how things went at the event?" A heavy sigh escaped her before she sank onto her seat.

"I'm sorry, Abs." He really was. She was right. He should have called her. But things had gone so well, and he'd gotten so lost in their private world. Then after, he'd been totally preoccupied with Patrick's problem with his brother.

"I was going bonkers all day yesterday wondering what happened."

"I totally suck as a best friend," he said.

"Yes!" She squared her shoulders. "You do." She hit him with her evil eye and sneered.

"How about I start making up for my thoughtlessness by sending you that picture you took of us, right now?" He snatched his phone from his desk, found the image, and hit AirDrop. Her phone beeped, and she checked the screen. She stared at her display, and a grin slowly brightened her face.

"That's a start," she drawled. "Taking me to lunch at that new Mediterranean restaurant in the Vista today would go a long way toward earning my complete forgiveness." She glanced up from under her lashes, a wicked gleam in her eyes.

"That can be arranged." He laughed. "I'd like to try the place, too."

"It's a date, then." She rolled closer to her desk and crossed her legs. "I want all the details at lunch." Abbie pointed a manicured finger in his direction. "Because that smile on your face tells me you had a *very* good time."

"Yes, I did." He couldn't help the smile. Most of their evening *had* been wonderful. "Saturday night was amaze—"

"Max!" His dad's bellow cut him off a second before the man himself rounded the corner. "In my office," he said, then pivoted and headed back down the hall.

"*Damn…*" Abbie mouthed the curse. "What's got him so riled up this early in the morning?"

"I'm about to find out." He groaned and pushed from his chair. What he didn't tell Abbie was that he already knew what had pissed his dad off: the charity event. More specifically, who he'd taken as his plus one.

His father was already in his office by the time Max caught up with him. But instead of finding the senior Segreti seated behind his desk, he found him leaning against the front, a newspaper clutched in his hand.

"Close the door," his father said.

Max did as instructed then faced his father. "What did you need to speak to me about?"

"No doubt that's a rhetorical question." His father stood, stalked forward, and slapped the newspaper against Max's chest. Max grabbed the paper before it fell. "You knew I'd see that this morning," he snapped. "You knew perfectly well photographers would be there."

Max stared down at the photograph in the center of the page. He and Patrick stood side-by-side smiling. His heart slammed against his sternum. He remembered that moment. Remembered the strong feel of Patrick's lower back against his palm as they'd waited for the camera's flash. The caption beneath the image read: Max Segreti and his partner, Patrick Guinness, former NFL player and local businessman.

His partner. Damn, he liked the sound of that. He couldn't help the stupid grin forming on his face.

"Oh, you think this is something to smile about?" his father snapped, and dropped into his seat. "You embarrassing your family and this firm makes you happy?"

"Taking a date to the event wasn't an embarrassment to you or anyone." Max marched forward and placed the paper onto the desk in front of his father.

"You know exactly what I'm talking about." He sneered. "Not only did you publicly put another man on your arm, but of all the men you could have chosen, you went with a *mechanic*." He surged from his chair and slammed his palms on the glass of his desk.

"So what!" Max matched the senior Segreti's stance. "He's a good man."

"Really?" His father straightened. "He's a good man, huh? That's what you think? Isn't this the same man whose brother is one of Gibson's clients? A seventeen-year-old arrested on drug charges?"

"They lost their dad, and his brother is going through a hard time right now," Max said, his temper rising. "Besides, Liam doesn't have a damn thing to do with this." It took everything he had not to tell his father to kiss his ass.

"You watch your mouth, young man."

"I'm a grown man!" His father needed to let this go before Max said something he'd regret. "And it's about time you realized that. I care a lot about Patrick. And who I have in my life is *my* decision."

"For God's sake." His father shook his head. "How long has this been going on?"

"Long enough."

"This man doesn't have a future, son." His father leaned back over his desk. "What will he bring to your relationship other than trouble, debt, and the complete absence of grandchildren to carry on our legacy?"

"That's enough," Max said between his teeth, his chest heaving. "You don't know what you're talking about."

"I know if you want to remain a part of this family, you'll drop this preposterous relationship." He lowered himself back onto his seat, as if the almighty patriarch had spoken and now all must heed his command.

Like hell.

"You're such a hypocrite," Max stated.

"What did you call me?" His father squared his shoulders and stuck out his chest, challenging him to say it again.

"You heard me," Max added. "You're a hypocrite. You donate to the unprivileged as if you actually care. But behind closed doors, you're an intolerant snob to those beneath your so-called status."

"How dare you stand there and criticize me after everything I've done for you." His father slowly rose. "It's my hard work, my money that has allowed you to have the best education at the best schools. Yet, you stand there and insult me." He inhaled deep. "You're fired," his father snapped.

Max recoiled. "What?"

"I said, you're fired," he repeated. "Now get out of my office."

Fury, hurt, and disappointment swirled inside him. Their sharp tentacles lashed out at his limbs, the sting from their cuts making him tremble. Nodding, Max uttered, "Fine. Maybe this is what we both need."

"For once, we agree," the senior Segreti said, his tone deep, final. He swiveled his chair in the opposite direction, facing the window, away from Max.

He'd been dismissed.

Permanently.

Max exited the office and closed the door behind him. His mind and body vacillated between completely numb and totally enraged. He'd been not only fired from the firm but disowned by his family.

Mindlessly, he pointed himself back toward his desk. Rounding the corner, he grabbed an empty banker's box sitting next to one of the multi-drawer file cabinets and dropped it on top of his desk.

"Finally," Abbie whispered, coming up behind him. "What happened? What was your father so fired up about?"

Doing his best to steady himself, Max drew in a deep breath and said, "Me."

"Oh, God." Abbie grasped his arm and faced him. "What happened?"

"Let's just say I've crossed an unacceptable line in his eyes, and for once, I'm not apologizing for it or backing down." Max collected the picture of his sister. He stared down at the sweet moment in time. Teresa had been ten years old when the photo was taken. He remembered because in the picture she was on her knees in the grass, hugging the one and only pet they'd been allowed to have—Grayson, a yellow lab. Christ, she'd loved that dog. But Grayson had been caught chewing on one of dad's shoes right after the dog had had an accident in the house. A slice of heartache carved its way through his chest, the pain tightening his grip on the metal frame. So as with everyone else in the family or business when they disappointed, Grayson had to go.

Saying good-bye to that dog had broken his little sister's spirit.

He stashed the framed image in the box, his jaw aching. Dammit, why had he waited so long to stand up to him?

"Max…?" Abbie's concerned voice cut through the haze of anger clouding his brain. "Max, what's going on?"

"What's going on is I've been fired," he said, and quickly tossed the rest of his few personal belongings into the box.

"You are fucking kidding me," she chewed out under her breath. "He can't do this!"

Max huffed and shook his head. "He can, and he did."

"You're his son, for Christ's sake."

Max shoved the lid to the box in place. "Since when has that ever mattered, Abbie? I've never been good enough for him."

"Oh my God," she breathed. "I don't know why it's taken me so long to figure out what's going on here. This is about Patrick, isn't it? It's because you took him to the charity event as your date."

"More like because I refused to stop seeing him," he said, curling his fingers into the box's handles and hoisting it from the desk.

"Good morning, you two," a deep voice interjected. Abbie turned and stepped to the side, allowing one of the partners to pass through.

"Good morning, Mr. Gibson," she said. "How are you

doing?"

"I'm fine," the tall, thin attorney said. "Max, how's it going? Not too many more months before the wait will finally be over on your results."

"It can't be soon enough, sir," Max said. Mr. Gibson passed, slapping Max on the shoulder and chuckling. Gibson was Liam's attorney, and the kid's case was coming up at the end of the week.

An idea bloomed inside Max's head.

If there was the slightest chance in hell Gibson would go for it, Max had to try. And he had only minutes to make the deal before his father would come storming out of his office to make sure he'd left the building.

"I'll be right back." Max shoved the box toward Abbie. She grabbed it, blinking.

"Where are you going?" she asked, her voice hushed.

"I need to talk to Mr. Gibson about a case."

Chapter Sixteen

"That's the first and last time I ever want to see you before a judge," Patrick said, passing through the kitchen.

"That makes two of us," Liam said, yanking open the fridge door. He grabbed a soda, popped the top, and closed the door.

"Please, Liam, take advantage of this opportunity to get your record eventually cleared by showing up for the community service and keeping your nose clean." Patrick dropped the mail on the counter.

"I told you I would. Geez. I'm not planning on screwing up." He took a sip from the red and white can. "But I have to give you props," he added. "I'm glad you hooked me up with that attorney. He was good."

"Yes, he was," Patrick said. "You have Max to thank for that recommendation, you know."

Patrick was beyond the point of missing the sexy-as-hell law grad. They hadn't talked since the night of the event. Granted, he hadn't called Max, either, since he'd been doing everything he could to mend the situation between him and

Liam, including cooling things between him and Max for a few days in hopes of giving Liam time to adjust. But he was about to go mad with the need to see him, to talk to him. And the new sensation had him off balance, unsettled, as if he had an itch he couldn't reach no matter how hard he tried.

A text had come in that morning from Max, wishing them a good outcome with Liam's case, but he kind of thought Max would have called by now.

Liam sighed, as he sank onto a seat at the kitchen table, drawing him back into the moment. "Don't remind me."

"Liam…" Patrick braced his palms on the laminated counter. "I thought we'd come to an understanding about Max and me over these last few days."

"You talked," Liam said, but his attention was focused on the window on the opposite wall. "I listened. That didn't mean I agreed with everything that came out of your mouth."

Groaning, Patrick left the kitchen and joined Liam at the table. How Dad had ever kept his sanity raising two boys, he would never understand. "Max is different, Liam."

His brother rolled his eyes, the move close to pissing him off.

"Yes, he comes from money," Patrick said, "and we don't. But Max is cool, and I'm starting to think that he and I might have a chance at making a relationship work."

Liam shrugged. "I still think you're blind as shit."

Patrick closed his eyes, praying for patience and the calm needed not to hit the kid with a left hook. "You're wrong. But I get where you're coming from. Hell, I had the same reservations. But—"

"You're in to him, and he gets you off," Liam bit out. "Oh, I completely understand."

"Dammit, kid," Patrick grumbled. "Can't you give me a break? I've done everything I can to get through to you. To make you happy. Can you talk to me for once with something more than a smartass comeback, please? Give me a clue about what I need to do."

Liam slammed his soda can on the table, carbonated liquid splattering across the wood. "I don't..." His breath hitched, and his hands fisted. "Shit! I'm scared, all right?" He glanced at Patrick, as if he were judging his reaction to the truth. "What if you find someone, and then you realize you want a permanent break? From me. I know I'm almost eighteen and everything..." He shook his head, his voice cracking, and the sound ripped a gaping hole in Patrick's heart. "But, what will happen to me then? I don't know if I'm ready to not have anyone." His dark eyes welled with unshed tears. "No family at all."

"Christ, Liam." Patrick's mind raced. He had no idea Liam felt so insecure. After losing their dad, the kid was scared to death of losing Patrick, too. "I'm always going to be there for you." He wrapped his hand over Liam's wrist, holding on to him tight. "You're my brother, and nothing can ever tear us apart. Even if I do meet someone that I want to make a part of my life, you and me, dude, we're forever. And whoever wants to be with me will just have to accept that fact or move on." Patrick risked a smile. "You feel me?" He tugged on Liam's arm.

Liam nodded. "You say that now..." He frowned. "But Max...you know he's going to want you all alone, not a package deal. Besides, he's got money, so I'm sure he has some kind of fancy place, and he would want you to move in there."

"You've been giving this way too much thought, brother." Patrick chuckled. "Number one, Max and I are not even close to thinking about any kind of permanent deal. Even if we were, Max isn't like that. He knows you're important to me. Plus, I don't think he'd care where we lived. He's not all about the rich life. Besides, no way would I move into his place like some charity case." Patrick stood and headed back to the kitchen counter. "We have a home."

Eyeing his brother, Patrick scooped the mail back up into his hand. "Are we good?" He glanced down at the envelopes.

"Yeah." Liam's chair squeaked as he got up. "We're good." The kid sighed and walked toward his room.

"I really hope so," Patrick called out, but he wasn't sure if Liam had heard him. Mainly the words were for his own reassurance.

Returning his attention to the mail, he noted one of the letters was from Segreti Law Firm. He opened the envelope and pulled out the documents. A check fluttered down onto the counter. He quickly scanned the figure and the paid to section. What the hell? Why would the firm be refunding Mr. Gibson's retainer?

He grasped the enclosed memo and read over the short paragraph. But only two words stood out: *pro bono.*

Since when had Gibson decided to handle Liam's case for free?

That hadn't been the original deal. Plus, why hadn't Gibson said something about that decision at the courthouse?

Then it hit him.

"No, no, no," he muttered under his breath. "He wouldn't…" Max wouldn't do that to him. His insides tightened. Because something down deep said that was precisely what had happened.

Patrick snatched his phone from the counter and quickly shot off a text. *Are you free? If so, I need to see you asap.*

It didn't take long for the phone to beep with Max's response, asking where he wanted to meet. After a couple more texts back and forth, they agreed to meet downtown in the park near the fountain.

Grabbing his keys, Patrick called out to his brother on his way to the door. "I'll be back later. I have to take care of something."

Maybe Liam replied? Maybe he didn't? Patrick didn't have time to wait around. If what he suspected had taken place, Max didn't understand who he was at all.

The noonday sun was baking the grass and pavement by the time Patrick arrived at the park. He'd grabbed the first vacant parking space and made his way to the area's focal point, the fountain. It had to be at least ninety-five degrees out, so the park wasn't crowded and he spotted Max right away. The dark-haired young attorney had nabbed one of the coveted benches near the water with partial shade.

Dressed in a pair of dark green cargo shorts, a white T-shirt, and sneakers, Max sat with one leg propped over the other, his foot shaking restlessly. With the temperature near triple digits, his clothing choice was appropriate, but it was odd to find him dressed so casual on a weekday. Even weirder, Patrick was the one in slacks and dress shirt for a change.

He strode to the bench. "New dress code for the Segreti Law Firm?"

Max looked up and sheepishly smiled. "No. I'm off today, and it's hot as hell out here."

"Yeah, it is." Patrick lowered himself onto the wood beside him, tugged at his neckline, and opened another button.

"It's really good to see you," Max said, his tone soft. "I've missed you."

"Same here." Patrick nodded. "I would have called you sooner, but Liam and I have been working through some things…"

"No problem." Max rested his forearms on his thighs, his fingers laced in front of him. "I understand. It's why I didn't call. I figured that was what was going on."

"Yeah. I think Liam really needed that time with me." God, this was awkward. Brutal as hell, actually. "Thanks for understanding," he added. Mentally groaning, he shoved a hand in his pocket and curled his fingers around the letter.

"How did things go in court?" Max shifted on the bench, facing him. "Is that why you wanted to see me? Shit." Worry creased his brow. "Please tell me it went well."

"It did," Patrick said. "Yeah. The attorney you recommended, Mr. Gibson, did a great job. Liam got probation along with community service, like we'd hoped." And there was his opening.

"That's great." Max smiled. "I'm happy things went as well as could be expected for him."

"Speaking of Mr. Gibson…" Patrick pulled the letter from his pocket along with the check. "Would you happen to know what this is all about?" He handed the documents over. With a look of confusion, Max opened the letter and scanned the contents.

"Oh, wow!" Max's eyes widened. "Tom decided to handle Liam's case pro bono. That's awesome." Max handed the papers back over, and Patrick absently accepted, his focus more on the other's man's expression than the action. "I imagine that was a pretty cool surprise."

Irritation stung Patrick's veins. Max was as cool as ice, but he wasn't giving the full story. He'd bet his last goddamn dime on it. Did Max really think he was that naive? "So this is how you're going to play it?"

"Excuse me?"

"This pro bono shit." Patrick held up the letter. "You're telling me you had no idea Gibson was going to do this." His heart thumped hard against his breastbone.

Max's posture straightened, tightened, as seconds quietly ticked away without a response. Patrick's fingers curled around the papers, the silence between them deafening despite the splashing waters of the fountain.

"You're angry," Max stated.

Angry? That wasn't the half of it. Embarrassed, disappointed, fucking pissed-off…he had a damn trifecta of emotions fighting for dominance inside, and that was just for starters. "Did you or did you not ask Gibson to do this?" he asked, each word carefully enunciated.

"I honestly thought this would be a relief—one less thing for you to have to worry about," Max said.

Something inside him broke—fractured in two. He could have sworn he heard the *pop* inside his head when Max uttered those words.

Leaning back against the bench, Patrick released a pathetic excuse for a laugh. "A relief?" He forced himself to face the other man. "I thought you knew me. Liam and I aren't one of the damn charity cases that you or your family need to save."

"I never thought that," Max snapped.

"Really?" He tossed the papers at his lover. "You could have fooled me."

"That's not what this was all about!"

"I don't need your pity," Patrick spat.

"Pity? You think I pity you?"

"We may not be as wealthy as the Segretis, but we can pay our bills." It was obvious that Max didn't see him as a man who could pull his own weight. He didn't need someone to take care of him. He wanted a partner, not a sugar daddy.

"You've got this all wrong." Max shook his head, his cheeks flushed.

"I don't think so." Patrick surged to his feet. Hell if he could sit there any longer. "How could there ever be anything more between us than what happens between the sheets if you don't see me as an equal? You going to Gibson like that, having the firm return my check…" Patrick stabbed the fingers of one hand through his hair, doing his best to keep it together. "You may as well have stamped a ticket on my time with you that said: services paid. I was nothing but a man whore."

"Patrick…" Max stood, his throat working. "There is a hell of a lot more between us than that, and you know it."

"Have I ever met your family?" Patrick shoved his hands into his pockets, needing something to hold onto. Max averted his gaze.

"That's more complicated than it sounds." Max crossed his arms, staring at some distant spot, away from him.

He understood introductions wouldn't have been easy, especially when it came to Maximo Sr. He knew Max's father hadn't completely come to terms with his son's sexuality. But if that were all it was, his father's issue with having to deal with the fact Max had a boyfriend, he'd have pushed the issue.

"Right," Patrick drawled, a bubbling pit of nausea growing in his stomach. Liam had been right all along. He scrubbed a palm across his mouth and jaw, swallowing hard against the bitter bile in the back of his throat. "You know," Patrick began, and Max glanced over at him. "I think trying to convince myself that we have a chance in hell of making this work is too complicated as well. So I'm done."

Patrick brushed past him, but he had no idea how with the overwhelming pain in his chest attempting to implode his heart.

"Patrick," Max called out. "Don't do this!"

But he didn't stop or look back. He couldn't. Not if he was going to be able to keep moving—to make it to the safety of his vehicle before he lost all sense and turned back around.

At last he made it to his truck, climbed inside, and slammed the door. His head banged against the back of the seat as he bashed his fist onto the driver's side door. In the sweltering heat of the cabin, sweat trickled down his temples, stinging his eyes. But he didn't give a shit. He didn't give a shit about anything. There was only one thing looping inside his mind.

"Thank God I never told him that I was falling in love with him," he whispered.

Chapter Seventeen

"Go away!" Max called out for the second time.

Dragging a pillow over his face, he groaned into the overstuffed fabric. The incessant pounding on his front door was driving him bonkers.

But instead of silence, the doorbell rang out.

Ding-dong. Ding-dong. Ding-dong.

There was only one person on the planet that could be this persistent when it was obvious he didn't want to talk to anyone: Abbie.

Max sighed, tossed the pillow onto the floor, and rolled off his couch. He trudged toward the door, and the bell rang out for what had to be the twentieth time.

"Give it a break already!" Max flipped the deadbolt and yanked open the door. As suspected, Abbie stood on the other side, wearing a pair of pale blue capris, a white blouse, and a pissed-off grimace.

"It's about damn time," she snapped and brushed past him into the condo. "You're lucky this manicure is two weeks old." She glanced are her nails. "Because the redo would have been going on your credit card."

"Excuse me, but I didn't want or ask you to go all Whack-a-Mole on my front door." He marched back to his spot on the couch and resumed his position. "As you can see, I'm alive. Now you can go." He looked up at her. "Shouldn't you be at work, anyway?"

"I'm on an extended break, and I'm not leaving until I get you out of this funk." She plopped onto the chair across from the couch. "It's been two weeks of this madness between you, Patrick, and your father, and I'm not taking it any longer."

"You have completely lost your mind, girl. How does any of this affect you?"

She groaned. "Please. Did you not leave me alone in that firm with your crazy father?"

"Oh. Yeah." He curled his lip. "Sorry about that."

"He's been hell on wheels since you left."

"You mean since I was fired." Max pushed from his supine position on the sofa and sat up against the cushion.

"It's my story." She shoved her hair back behind her ear. "Don't nitpick." Abbie stood and headed to the kitchen. "You have any coffee in this place? I haven't had my quota of caffeine yet today."

"I think so. I don't remember the last time I stopped by the store or made any. Check the cabinet above the coffeemaker."

"Found it," she called out, and started clattering around on the other side of the wall. About ten minutes later, she returned with two mugs. Despite the fact he hadn't asked for any, she set one cup in front of him then returned to her chair.

Max glared at his friend, making sure his best "I'm annoyed" face was in full effect. Tendrils of aroma permeated his space, and yeah, the coffee did smell delicious. His stomach growled, and his mouth watered. *Fuck it.* Begrudgingly, he reached for the cup.

Abbie smirked. "I knew you couldn't resist."

"Bite me." He took a sip of the hot brew.

"Wouldn't you rather a certain former NFL player sink his teeth into you?"

Sharp pain arrowed through his sternum at the mention of his ex. *Shit!* He choked back a wince. "Don't go there," he said, his voice hoarse.

"Come on, Max," she drawled. "You're miserable. Why don't you call him? Try to talk to him."

"No." He plopped his mug onto the table, the bottom of the ceramic mug releasing a *crack* off the wood. "He doesn't want to hear from me."

"How do you know that if you don't try?"

"I know." He glanced at his friend. "Believe me. My voice is the last thing he wants to hear."

"If you say so," she said, followed by a sigh. "But Liam came by the office right before I left."

"He did?" Kudos to Abbie. She'd managed to nab his attention. "What for?"

"He was looking for you." She edged forward on her seat and placed her mug onto the table with his. "Funny thing is… he had no idea you didn't work for the firm any longer."

"What did you tell him?" he asked, making sure he played it cool.

"The truth, of course."

Needing to move, he stood. The damn place was huge, but somehow he still felt trapped. Caged. He'd already paced every square inch of the condo, repeatedly.

"If you wanted me to feed Liam or Patrick a different story, you should have told me," she added.

"No. You shouldn't have to lie for me."

"Why didn't you tell Patrick what happened between you and your father?"

"I didn't really get a chance." He stared out the window into the parking lot, watching the cars come and go. "And by the time I might have been able to say something, it was too late. Patrick had already made his mind up about me—about us. Besides, I wasn't about to tell him that my father had fired me for the exact reason why Patrick claimed we couldn't be together." He turned, facing Abbie. "So you can see why going into the details about my firing wasn't going to help a damn thing."

"But he might have understood where your head was at the time," she said.

His stomach twisted once more. "Patrick was too hurt to listen to anything I had to say." Releasing a heavy sigh, he crossed his arms. "I did that. No way around it. Whether or not I was still reeling from the blowout I'd had with my father, in the end, I hurt him."

He returned to couch and plopped back down onto his spot.

"If you're not going to talk to Patrick, then…" She inhaled deep. "I can't believe I'm about to say this, but I really believe you should talk to your father."

A lash of anger surged through him. "What? What do I have to say to him? Because of him I lost the man I—" He bit back the word. If he said it aloud, he might lose it. Break apart. And he wasn't sure if he'd ever put the pieces back the same way again.

"Love?" Abbie finished for him. "Don't you think you need to tell your father those words? That Patrick's the man you love."

The idea of expressing that to his father…that he'd give a damn that his son was in love and that it would actually make a difference was almost too bizarre to imagine.

She stood, maneuvered around the coffee table, and sat down beside him. Wrapping an arm around his shoulder, she continued, "Believe it or not, based on how crazy your father's been acting at work, I really think he loves you and misses you."

"You can't be serious." He scoffed.

"I bet your mom has been trying to call you and tell you the same thing, too."

On that, she was right. He nodded. His mom had been blowing up his phone with messages about calling his father.

"I think now that you two have had some time to cool down, maybe he'll listen to you. Take this opportunity and try to get your father to see how much Patrick means to you. Tell him that if he wants you in his life, he needs to be willing to accept all of you, not just the parts he's comfortable with."

She made a good point. *Damn...* He looked over at her. "Who are you and what have you done with my friend?"

She laughed.

"How and when did you become so mature — and smart?" He smirked.

"From hanging around you." She grinned. "Well, except when it comes to your father and your love life. With that, you kind of need some help."

"You think?" He rocked sideways, bumping her shoulder, and they laughed.

"So why don't you go take a shower, shave, get dressed, and come back to the office with me?"

The thought sent a cold thread of dread through his veins, but she was right. He had to face his father. Living like this — avoiding his mother's calls, the incessant unease inside him because of the huge yawning rift between him and his father — was miserable. And after listening to what Abbie had to say, he realized that he didn't want to face another day without having tried to come to an understanding with him.

"Go on and head back," he said. "I need time to think about a few things before I leave. But I'll be there."

"You promise?" She eyed him, doubt written in her expression.

"I'll be there." He nodded. "I promise."

"Okay." She stood, bent over, gave him a quick hug. "I'm so glad you're going to talk to him."

"Me, too," he said, and he meant it. Even though he didn't know if he had a chance in hell of making a difference, he had to try. Maybe he could save his relationship with at least one of the men in his life.

• • •

Two o'clock rolled around whether he was ready for it or not. Showered and dressed in his business casual attire, Max felt almost human again. Sitting in his car, he studied the profile of the building that housed his father's law firm, running over the things he wanted to say if and when his father agreed to see him. His cell rang out from where he'd placed it in the console between the seats. Grabbing it, he checked the display. His eyes widened and his heart stuttered at the name staring back at him: Father.

"What the hell?" he whispered.

Too curious to resist, especially since he was sitting in the parking lot, he tapped *answer*. "Hello?"

"I wasn't sure you'd pick up," his father replied. "I was prepared to leave a message."

"Is everyone okay?" Max worked the gearshift under his palm.

"Everyone is fine. But you'd know that if you'd answered a single one of your mother's calls. She's worried about you, Max."

"Is that why you're calling? To demand I call my mother?"

"No," his dad said. "That's not what this is about."

"What is it about, then?"

"I was hoping you could stop by the firm this afternoon," he said.

"Really?" *What, does he want to tell me in person that he is striking me from his will?* "Why?"

"Because I think it's about time you and I talked," his dad said, his voice deep and solemn. "This silence between us isn't doing either one of us any good."

Shit. The man had pushed his stubborn pride aside and called him first.

"I couldn't agree with you more," Max said.

"When can you come by?" His dad's tone lifted.

"How about now? The timing of your call was kind of perfect. I'm actually right outside."

"You're here? Are you meeting Abbie?"

"No." He swallowed hard. "I came to talk to you."

Moments later, Max opened the glass doors of the firm and crossed the threshold. No longer a key card-carrying member of the place, he was relegated to entering via the front like the rest of the population. And it was strange as hell.

Walking up to the front desk, he spotted Abbie through the glass. She hit the buzzer to the interior door, allowing him access to the back office.

"Hey there." She swiveled in her chair to face him. "It's really good to see you here."

"Feels weird come through this way."

"Even stranger having to buzz you in," she said and stood, closing the distance between them. "Did you call your father and tell him you were coming? He just rang me to tell me to send you on back when you come in."

"No. Believe it or not, he actually called me when I was in the parking lot."

"What?" Her brows lifted. "I guess miracles do still occur."

"I'm now a believer."

She patted his arm and headed back to her desk.

Max followed the familiar hallway down to his father's

office. After he gave a one-two rap on the door, his dad called out, "Enter."

Stepping inside, Max said, "Hey." The door swung shut behind him. "It's me."

His father sat on the other side of the mammoth desk. Glancing up from his paperwork, he lowered his pen to the glass and leaned back.

"I can see that." His father threaded his fingers and rested his elbows on the arms of his chair. "Come have a seat."

Max picked one of the two padded leather armchairs in front of the desk. Crossing one leg on top of the other, he settled back and tried to make himself as comfortable as possible, considering he was about to confront probably the best attorney in the state.

Sighing, his dad rocked forward and folded his arms. "So how long is this nonsense of you not working for the firm going to go on?"

Well, that didn't put him immediately on the defensive at all. "Probably as long as you continue to feel that I'm a stain on our family and this firm."

"Max," his dad rumbled. "You're turning this fissure between us into the damn Grand Canyon."

"You think *I'm* the one overreacting?" Each beat of Max's heart slammed into his throat. It had been less than five minutes, and the top of his head was already about to blow. "How else do you think I should've responded to your demand that I stop seeing the man in my life or else you'd disown me?"

"You blatantly defied me, showing up with him," his father snapped. "You forced my hand."

"I forced your hand..." he seethed. "I was seen with a date in public, and it was too much for you to handle." Max shoved from his chair. He couldn't sit there any longer or he was going to go mad. "Do you hear yourself?"

"We have to think of the firm and its reputation," his father bellowed.

"The firm will survive," Max slapped his palms on the desk, closing some of the distance between them. "But I won't, Dad," he said, lowering his voice. "I can't live like this any longer. I want to be in your life, a real part of our family and the business, but I need you to accept all of me." He inhaled a shaky breath. "Not just the parts most palatable to your sensibilities."

His father sat in silence, unmoving. Max had no idea if that was a good sign or a bad one. He stepped back toward his chair and sank onto the seat, his arm and legs suddenly weak.

"I realized something, though, through all of this," Max began again. "I'm in love with Patrick Guinness."

That got his dad's attention. His eyes widened, and he straightened in his chair.

"No matter how far you decide to take my banishment, it won't change how I feel about Patrick. Or who I am. I'm a gay man, Dad. I'm a gay man who's in love." He allowed that idea to sink in for a moment. "I can tolerate losing my job, my place here at the firm…" His voice cracked. *Dammit.* He tightened his fingers around the arms of his chair, needing to hold on to something steady. He would finish this strong. "But what I can't tolerate is living without Patrick."

He was never giving up on the big guy. Coming here today had somehow renewed his hope in what he and Patrick had. No matter what, he'd find a way to win Patrick back. He had to. Because the damn guy was the other half of his soul.

He lifted a brow at his father, an unspoken *you're up, counselor.*

"I take it you're finished?" He cocked his head in Max's direction.

Max nodded.

"Looks like all that money wasn't wasted on your law

degree, son."

Seriously? Max sighed.

"You made a good case." The elder gentlemen rocked forward once more. "I had no idea your feelings ran that deep for this man."

"They do."

"I also hadn't fully realized how much my rigidity about your..."

"My sexuality?" Max lifted his brow.

"Yes." His father nodded. "How much pain I'd caused you." A long exhale exited his dad, as if he were finally releasing a heavy burden from his shoulders. "As much as it chafes me to acknowledge this, your mother was right. This is my fault." He repositioned, the chair's leather squeaking beneath him. "Somehow I got it in my head that as long as I didn't see you in a relationship with another man, I didn't have to accept it." His Adam's apple bobbed. "Maybe I thought if enough time passed, you'd fall in love with a woman and start a family."

"It doesn't work that way, Dad. No amount of time is going to change me. And believe it or not, I'm happy with exactly who I am."

"I'm beginning to understand that." He swiped a hand over his salt-and-pepper hair, the strands unmoving from the amount of product his dad had applied. "I think it's time I reveal something to you about my past. Maybe then you can gain some small amount of understanding about me."

"Okay. I'm listening." He couldn't believe the turn of their conversation. He was about to open up to Max, reveal a part of his childhood. In his whole life, his father had never really talked to him. He truly couldn't remember a time when he'd shared a father-son moment with the man. His pulse kicked up a notch. *Shit.* Inside, he was damn near giddy.

"I've never told you or your sister anything about your

grandfather beyond the fact that he died a few decades ago. In fact, I've never revealed to anyone other than your mother that he'd been a mentally and physically abusive SOB."

"Oh my God." Stunned, Max scooted forward onto the edge of his seat. "Why didn't you say something?"

"There was no reason for you or Teresa Anne to know. I had no intentions of ever repeating history with my own children. And as far as I was concerned, your grandfather and his memory needed to stay buried." He breathed deep, as if the extra oxygen gave him the strength to carry on. "Yet, despite my best efforts, a few of his undesirable traits reared their ugly heads through me. Your mother has been trying to make me face my demons for years, especially after you and I argued."

"I see," Max whispered. He'd been a complete idiot, ignoring his mother's calls. But he'd believed she'd only try and make excuses for his father, like always. All these years, he'd believed his mother had been weak, blind to his father's actions. But behind the scenes, she'd been trying to help, doing everything she could to get their father to see the pain he'd been causing.

"Your grandfather was a complete hard-ass who dominated his family." His father barked a laugh. "Dear God." He shook his head and closed his eyes. "Sound familiar?"

"Maybe this is too soon," Max said, despite the painful band wrapped around his chest, restricting his ability to breathe. "But I have to ask. Do you think it's possible for you to find a way to come to terms with who I am?"

His father looked up, and for once, instead of cold indifference staring back at him, Max found pain and something resembling compassion in the other man's eyes.

"I've always loved you, Max," his father said. "And I'm sorry if I ever made you feel inadequate. I'm the one with the problem. Not you," his father bit out. "My pride, my unceasing concern over this firm and our status in the community, almost drove you away." He shook his head. "Damn it all to hell. None of this is worth losing my son." His voice turned gravelly. "So yes, in answer to your question, I definitely believe that it's possible."

Behind a veil of unshed tears, Max's vision blurred. His heart swelled, rupturing the band around his rib cage. He'd never expected to hear those words in his lifetime.

"If you can forgive an old man for his outdated views," his father added, "I would also love to have you back here where you belong."

After the breakthrough he and his father had just experienced, that decision was a no-brainer.

"I would like very much to come back," Max said, a smile tugging at his mouth. "As long as who I date isn't going to be issue, including if that person is Patrick?"

"I will do my best to keep my opinions to myself," his father said. "But keep in mind, I'm a work in progress. Old dogs, new tricks, as they say."

Max stood and stretched out his hand. His father slid his palm into Max's for a firm shake. No, it wasn't a hug. But honestly, if his father had wanted to embrace, Max would have been freaked out by the overly enormous shift in personality.

But hey, his father admitting he'd been too rigid, and accepting the fact that his son was gay…huge milestone.

It was a good day.

Chapter Eighteen

Damn, he was going to feel this last set.

Patrick's triceps screamed as he pumped the twenty-pound weight up and down behind his head for... Hell, if he could remember how many reps. Not that it mattered. He'd stop when his muscles decided to do it for him.

"Hey, bro!" Liam called out from the front of the house. "You home?"

"Yeah!" Patrick's arm locked, his triceps exhausted. He grunted, lowered his arm, and dropped the weight to the bedroom floor. "I'm back here."

Opening and closing his fingers, he shook out his limp arm. A dull throb radiated throughout the extremity. *Good.* At least when he worked out until his body ached he could focus on something besides the pain behind his sternum.

For the last couple of weeks—after his blow up with Max—work was all that his days and nights had consisted of. He showed up at the shop in the mornings and buried himself in whatever car, truck, or paperwork he could find. After closing, he kept himself busy working out. If his body was moving, he didn't have time to think. If his limbs ached like a mother, he didn't have to feel the shit inside.

"Hey." Liam poked his head into the room. "I brought home some burgers if you're interested," he said, and quickly darted back out. But not before Patrick noticed the dark shadow under his brother's eye.

He may have been distracted the last couple of weeks, but he wasn't so disconnected that he didn't recognize a blow to the face when he saw one.

Patrick stood up from his position on the edge of the bed and tracked the other guy to the kitchen. "Hold up," he called out.

Liam held the door to the refrigerator open. "What's up?" he asked, but kept his back to Patrick.

"Come here," Patrick ordered.

"Why? I'm getting something to drink. You want something?"

"Not right now. What I want is for you to close the fridge and come over here so I can get a closer look at what you're trying to hide."

Groaning, Liam closed the door. "It's nothing. Really."

"Then let me get a look at nothing."

"Fine." Liam huffed then plodded over to where Patrick stood by the kitchen table.

Even though he was still a couple of feet away, Patrick could make out the bruise on his brother's cheekbone, as well as the black and blue wrapping itself around his eye. "What the hell happened?" When Liam stopped in front of him, Patrick leaned in for a closer look. "How's your vision? Any blurriness? Pain?"

"It's okay." He backed away, plopped down in front of the bag of food he'd brought home, and placed his can of soda on the table. "I told you, I'm fine."

His brother might not be permanently injured, but he

wasn't fine, either. "Talk to me, Liam. What went down?" Patrick glanced at the McDonald's bag. "You apparently showed up at work, so how did you end up with a black eye? Were you attacked by a Big Mac?"

Liam glared at him from under his lashes. "God, you're such a comedian." He grabbed his soda and downed a gulp before continuing. "A couple of guys I knew from school showed up there tonight. They were hanging around outside when I got off."

Patrick pulled out a chair and claimed a spot across from his brother. "Okay," he said. "What did they want?"

A wave of anger flashed across Liam's face, flushing his cheeks. "They wanted to make sure they were there to watch when I spotted the message they'd left for me on my rear windshield."

"Oh, fuck," Patrick groaned. Anger and nausea churned in the pit of his stomach. "What did it say?"

"They wrote 'Fag Brothers, Inc.' in big fat white letters on the glass."

"Bastards!" Fury raced through Patrick's core, sending his heart rate soaring. He flexed his fingers, visions of choking those assholes flashing through his mind. "I can't believe this shit," he growled. "Jesus! You just started your probation. Because of those creeps, you could've ended up back behind bars for getting in a fight."

"I know." Liam groaned. "But it wasn't so much that they'd written that crap on my windshield. I can wash the glass, and I can take whatever they want to say about me. But they started running their mouths about you and Max, and fuck…it pissed me off!"

"Me and Max?" Patrick frowned.

"I guess after the story and pictures of you and Max ended up in local paper, word's gotten around about you two," Liam said.

"Damn. I'm so sorry you ended up hurt over something I did." Fucking hell. The urge to punch the shit out of someone rode him hard.

"It's not your damn fault. It's theirs." He huffed. "Like I said, I can handle them and their bullshit. I've been letting that crap roll off my back for years. But you're my damn brother! I can talk trash about you, but no one else has the right to." Liam took another sip of his soda.

"I appreciate you wanting to stick up for me. But I'm surprised at you getting all worked up about me and Max. You know we're ancient history. And you didn't even like him."

"Maybe I didn't." Liam shrugged. "But you did." Staring at his soda, Liam rotated the can with his fingertips. "And you still do. You guys are *so* far from ancient history."

Where is this coming from? "Max and I are finished."

"I stopped by the Segreti Law Firm this morning." He glanced up at Patrick.

"Why the hell did you do that?"

"I wanted to talk to Max," he said, deflecting his attention back to his can. "You've been miserable ever since you two broke up. And I've never seen you happier than when you were with him." He looked back over at Patrick. "He made you happy, and I wanted to try and help to fix things between you guys. Especially since I'm partly to blame for screwing things up."

Patrick swallowed hard against the fist in this throat that threatened to choke him. "Why we broke up had nothing to do with you, Liam. You hear me? Why we're not seeing each other anymore is *not* your fault."

"Did you know Max was fired?" Liam asked, abruptly dismissing the subject.

"What?" Patrick blinked, trying to make sense of what his brother had said. "Who told you that?"

"Abbie. You know, the woman at the front desk that you said was a friend of Max's."

"Shit," he breathed. "Did she say when?"

"A couple of weeks ago." Liam pulled one of the burgers from the bag. "She said his father let him go right after you two went to that fancy charity event."

Stunned, Patrick slid his forearms onto the table, needing the sturdy feeling of the wood. Why hadn't Max said anything? His head spun. Then it hit him. Of course… Abbie said he'd lost his job after the charity event, which meant Max hadn't told him because the reason his father fired him had something to do with Patrick.

That had to be it.

"Son of a bitch," Patrick muttered. "Talk about a fucking tangled web."

"What'd you say?" Liam mumbled around his mouthful of hamburger.

"Nothing." Patrick shook his head. "Just talking to myself."

"They say that's the first sign of insanity." His brother stuffed his mouth with another bite.

"Kiss my ass." Patrick stood.

"I'm just saying." He shrugged. "Giving you a heads-up."

"Yeah, right." Patrick nabbed a burger from the bag. "You're such a wealth of knowledge." He strode into the kitchen and grabbed a beer from the fridge. On the way back to his room, he gave his brother's shoulder a light tap. "By the way, even though you were out of line, I appreciate what you were attempting to do."

"No big deal." Liam glanced up at him. "Like I said, if Max really makes you happy, man, you should go for it. To hell with what everyone else thinks—including me."

"But I do care what you think." Liam was his family, and his feelings mattered, especially while they shared a roof.

"When are you going to learn to ignore what comes out of my mouth?" Liam quirked a smile. "I'm an idiot half the time."

Patrick laughed. "Your words, dude. Not mine."

"Call him, Pat." Liam pulled another burger from his McDonald's haul. "You know you want to."

Patrick cocked his head, hitting his brother with a *you think you know it all* glare.

"Don't look at me like that, you jerk," Liam spat. "Call him and invite him out. Get over yourself so you two can kiss and make up." His brother puckered his lips, making kissing sounds at him.

Patrick grimaced. "Don't make me gag."

He made his way back toward his room with Liam's laughter filling the air. His brother had a good soul. He'd been targeted by bullies tonight, yet what had sent him over the edge and into a fight was the fact the other guys had been talking trash about him and Max. Patrick sank onto the side of his bed, pride for his brother swelling inside.

Damn, it irritated the hell out of him, but the kid was so on target. He'd been going out of his mind missing Max, and he needed to talk to him.

Grabbing his cell off the nightstand, he pulled his legs up onto the mattress and sat back against the headboard. Bringing up his favorites list in his contacts, he tapped on his former lover's name. Max's number and info filled the display, and his insides did that weird flip-flop thing at the sight.

Step one down.

Now if he could only figure out how this conversation was supposed to go.

He tapped the number, and the phone began to dial.

Fuck it. Nothing like diving in headfirst and figuring out the rest later.

"Hello…Patrick?"

Max's deep voice washed over and through him, heating him from the inside out. God, how he missed him.

"Yeah," he said, but the word came out all scratchy sounding. He cleared his throat. "It's me."

"Wow. It's bizarre that you called," Max said. "I was actually about to call you."

"You were?" His stomach flipped. "What about?"

"Abbie mentioned that Liam came by the office today."

"Right. He did. We were actually just talking about it." The line fell silent, and he couldn't help but wonder if Max was waiting on him to say the words first. If so, why keep the guy in suspense any longer? "Liam told me that you were fired."

"Yeah. Things between me and my father were rocky for a while."

"Why didn't you tell me?" *Christ.* Part of him felt like a complete ass for questioning why Max hadn't spilled his guts right away about being fired. Because deep down, he knew why. That would be his highness, the king of overreaction: Patrick Guinness. The level at which he'd blown up that day in the park… He closed his eyes. Shit. He'd acted like a fool.

"I know, and I'm so damn sorry, PG. There's a lot I want to talk to you about. Things you need to know, if you'll give me the chance. I know I hurt you by going to Gibson…I hadn't thought it through when I did that."

"Stop," Patrick said. "Stop taking all the blame here. There's more than enough of it to go around." Emotions rocked through him like he was a ship adrift in a storm, its hull being bashed by an angry sea. Max hadn't set out to make him feel like less of a man. In his heart, Patrick knew that had never been his intention.

"It's me who screwed up," Patrick found himself saying. "And I've spent the last couple of weeks doing everything possible to exorcise you from my head."

"How's that been going for you?" Max asked. "Because for me, I haven't been able to forget you. Not for one damn second."

Patrick squeezed his eyes shut and choked back a moan. He missed Max so damn bad that he didn't care if he ever heard the full story. Because all along, the only thing that'd been in the way of them being together was his own damn issues. And he finally got that.

He wanted Max back. He wanted him in his arms now. Not tomorrow at some damn restaurant, sitting across a fucking table.

"It hasn't worked—I can't—I don't know how to do this…" *Without you*, he wanted to say, but the words were stuck in his throat. Where in the hell had his head been when he broke things off?

Damn his stupid Guinness pride! It had nearly cost him everything.

"You're all I can think about," Max said. "Every time I close my eyes, you're there. Every morning when I open them again, you're my first thought."

Max was killing him. Each declaration went straight through his heart, punching holes through the already wounded organ. He was bleeding out, and Max was the only person capable of patching him up, putting him back together again. God help him, he loved Max. And he'd never stopped loving him.

"When do you want to meet?" The question fell from his tongue before he'd realized he'd formed the words.

"If you're free, how about I send a car for you tomorrow night around eight?"

"A car?" That was odd. "Where are we meeting that you'd need to send a car?"

"Is that a yes?"

"I'm free," Patrick said. "But you didn't answer my

question."

"I know I'm asking a lot after what we've gone through lately, but trust me. I think this will be the perfect place," Max said, and Patrick could hear the smile in his voice.

With no choice but to go with whatever Max had planned, Patrick relented. "Can you at least tell me how I should dress?"

"Whatever you wear will be fine. Just come dressed as Patrick Guinness. That's all I care about."

"Then that's what you'll get," Patrick said.

"See you tomorrow," Max said, his voice hushed.

"Tomorrow." Patrick tapped *end call* and checked the time. How the hell was he supposed to pass the next twenty-four hours and not go mad?

• • •

Somehow Patrick had managed to pull off a couple of hours of restless sleep. Most of the night he'd lain awake, replaying his last conversation with Max over and over in his mind.

The hum of an engine in front of his house alerted him that Max's hired car had finally arrived. Grabbing his wallet from the counter, he shoved it in the back pocket of his pants. As Max had requested, he'd dressed in the clothes that made him comfortable—black denim, boots, and a dark green button-down shirt tucked into the waistband of his jeans.

A knock sounded at the door, and Patrick made his way over to answer it. A chauffeur dressed in a black business suit stood on the other side of the threshold.

"Mr. Guinness?"

"That would be me, I guess," Patrick said.

"Mr. Segreti sent me to pick you up," he said.

"I'm ready." Patrick switched off the interior lights, stepped outside, and locked the door. Liam was working again this evening, but Patrick told him about his plans tonight before he'd left. It shocked the hell out of him—again—when the kid told him he was happy that he and Max were going to meet. His brother never stopped surprising him.

Patrick climbed in the back of the limo, and the driver closed the door. The smell of leather and glass cleaner filled Patrick's nostrils as the car pulled away and entered the flow of traffic.

"Where are we headed?" Patrick called out to the driver.

"I'm sorry, sir, but Mr. Segreti instructed me to only take you to his location, not to answer any questions."

"Wow, seriously?" *Well, damn.* What was the nerd up to?

"Make yourself comfortable, sir. We'll be there in about twenty minutes."

Patrick settled back into the seat and attempted to lose himself in the passing scenery. But his mind wouldn't stop racing, wouldn't stop looping the words Max had said toward the end of their last conversation.

"There's a lot I want to talk to you about, things you need to know."

"You're all I can think about. Every time I close my eyes, you're there. Every morning when I open them again, you're my first thought."

Grunting, Patrick shifted in his seat. Could the car move any damn slower?

After what had felt like hours, the driver tapped the turn signal and they veered into one of the upscale neighborhoods outside the city limits.

"Where are you taking me, Blue Eyes?" Patrick whispered.

The driver made another couple of turns, taking them deeper into the community, breezing past one gorgeous estate after another. Had Max decided to lease an entire estate home for their meeting-slash-date?

Over the top much, Max?

On a street lined with palmetto trees, crepe myrtles, and dogwoods, they finally turned onto a brick-paved driveway. The pavers circled in front of a large stone-and-stucco home. The limo rolled to a stop a few feet away from a sidewalk that weaved a path to a massive pair of red, arched, double front doors. Patrick glanced out the left side of the car where a triple-tiered fountain bubbled. A stone Grecian goddess stood at the top, pouring water from a pitcher in her hand. The brightly lit waterfall landed in a bowl beneath her feet then cascaded over its sides, over and over again, until it filled a mammoth-size well at the base.

"Where the hell have you had me delivered, Blue Eyes?" he asked himself.

The car door opened, and the chauffeur motioned for him to exit. "Mr. Segreti is waiting for you inside, sir."

"Thank you," Patrick said, and proceeded along the red-and-black speckled brick. At the door, he started to knock, but before he made contact, Max swung it open.

"You're here," Max said, a brilliant smile lighting up his eyes.

Gorgeous.

And just like that, Patrick forgot how to breathe. Max stood in the doorway dressed in a white button-down dress shirt tucked into a pair of dark blue slacks. Nothing fancy. Yet on Max, the look was a class act. It took every ounce of Patrick's control not to yank Max into his arms and kiss him until they'd both erased every last memory of why they'd ever been apart.

"Yeah. We're both here," Patrick said, forcing himself to focus on what he'd come to do—talk to Max. "But do you mind finally telling where exactly 'here' is?"

"My pleasure."

Max stepped forward, closing a few inches of the distance between them, taking him by surprise. His hand slid into

Patrick's and gently squeezed. The sensation went straight to Patrick's head, knocking him off kilter.

"Come with me," Max said.

Still reeling from the other man's touch, all he could do was follow. Max guided him through a two-story round foyer and down a hall lined with pictures, but they were moving too quickly for Patrick to make out the faces inside the frames. At the end of the corridor, the space opened up again, and they entered a large living room. Max stopped a few steps inside the room, with Patrick at his side. Movement stirred to their left, drawing Patrick's attention.

Max had failed to mention they wouldn't be alone this evening.

"Everyone," Max said, giving his hand another squeeze, grounding him.

A man who appeared to be somewhere in his fifties stood, followed by a woman around the same age, and then a girl who probably hadn't been out of high school for very long moved into sight.

"Mom, Dad, Theresa, I'd like you to meet Patrick Guinness."

Max's family?

Shock rolled through him with tsunami force, and if it hadn't been for the stabilizing grip of Max's hand, he would've stumbled.

What the fucking hell?

Without one single damn warning, Max had brought him to his parent's home.

Max turned to him with an unmistakable fierce look of resolve in his eyes. "Patrick's my boyfriend," he stated.

Maybe the shock of the whole moment had rattled his brain. But he could have sworn Max had just announced to his family that Patrick was his boyfriend.

The next moment, Max's dad stood in front of him. "It's

nice to meet you, Patrick." Mr. Segreti stuck out his palm. His words were warm, welcoming, but the offer of his hand had come off a little stiff, hesitant. However, he had to give the man credit for playing it cool for his son. He appeared to be trying.

Max released his hold on Patrick's hand, prompting Patrick to snap out of his thoughts.

"Likewise, sir." Patrick placed his hand inside the other man's and shook.

"Patrick," Max's mom called out. "I'm so glad Max invited you for dinner so we could get to know you."

Dinner? He'd invited him over to sit at a table and eat with his whole family. Patrick risked a quick glance at Max, who stood there looking like the cat that had captured, toyed with, then swallowed the canary. If he didn't love the guy so much, he'd take him outside and strangle him.

"Can I get you something to drink, dear?" Max's mom patted Patrick's arm.

"No, thank you, Mrs. Segreti. I'm good for now."

"Hey," Max's sister said, strolling over to take her turn at him. She was a beautiful girl, about an inch or two shorter than Max, with amber eyes like her father and hair the same color and wavy texture as her brother's. Her red dress flowed around her legs as she approached him, and her hair hung loose midway down her back. "I'm Teresa, if you haven't figured that out by the process of elimination yet."

"Nice to meet you."

"Wow. I can't believe I'm actually speaking to one of Max's boyfriends live and in the flesh. And in this house."

"One of Max's boyfriends?" Patrick cocked an eyebrow in Max's direction.

"My only current boyfriend," Max interjected.

"It's going to probably be another twenty or thirty more minutes on dinner," his mom said. "Why don't you show

Patrick around, Max? My favorite part of the house is the sunroom. It faces the rear of the property."

"Sure," Max said. "Would you like a short tour, Patrick?"

"That sounds great." It actually sounded amazing. He'd have Max all to himself for more than a minute so he could ask him, "What the fuck?"

"Cool," Max said. "Follow me."

Patrick trailed Max out of the room, and after passing what looked like a library, then an office, they entered a large, rectangular room with floor-to-ceiling windows. The view looked out over an immaculate lawn and pool. Before Max could utter another word, Patrick grabbed his arm, spinning him around and putting them face-to-face.

"I can't believe you brought me here for dinner with your whole family without any warning," Patrick said, his voice hushed.

"I'm sorry about the big surprise," Max said. "Well, kind of."

"Kind of sorry?"

"I wanted to make sure you knew without a doubt that there was nothing keeping us apart any longer." Max reached up and cupped Patrick's cheek. "There are no barriers. No more secrets. I want everything out in the open. And what better way to show you than to do the one thing I'd never had the balls to do before: introduce you to my family."

"You certainly got my attention. But what changed with your father?"

"Everything."

Max told him about their confrontation, and how the walls between them had crumbled.

"That's awesome," Patrick said. Damn, Max had nerves of steel. He didn't think it was possible, but fuck, he loved him even more.

"I'm sorry about how I went off on you in the park,"

Patrick continued. "I wasn't the only one who'd been hurt that day, and you didn't deserve my anger." Patrick shook his head, clearing his throat. He had to get this out. "I acted like an idiot, Max. Asking Gibson to take Liam's case pro bono was…you being you. A damn nice guy."

"It's okay, PG." Max placed a palm over Patrick's heart. "You had no idea what had happened between me and my father."

"No, dammit." Patrick shook his head and clamped his hand around Max's. "You wanted to help us. That was all there was to it. You didn't go to him thinking of me as a man who couldn't take care of his family. And I needed to get that through my thick head."

"You're not still irritated with me about tonight?" Max's smile turned sheepish.

"No." Patrick chuckled. "I'm glad I've met your family."

"Good." The warmth of Max's arm wrapped around him. "Now, please kiss me before I jump out of my skin."

It was about damn time.

Patrick sealed his mouth over Max's and every neuron inside him sparked to life. Driving inside Max's mouth, he stroked the other man's tongue with his, and he couldn't hold back a groan of pleasure. The missing part of his heart, his soul, had been found.

Breaking away, he gasped and rested his forehead against Max's. "Christ, I've missed you."

"I thought I was going to lose my mind waking up each day knowing I wouldn't see you—touch you," Max said.

Patrick cupped Max's face, lifting the other man's gaze to his. "I love you, Max Segreti," he said, his voice raw.

"Oh, fuck," Max uttered.

Panic seized Patrick's heart. Too soon. *Shit.* He didn't want to push him. "You don't have to say it back," he said, scrambling to hold it together. "I just needed you to know."

"It's okay." Max chuckled. "It's really okay. I think my brain kind of had a meltdown when you said what you said."

"When I said that I love you." His heart rate settled back down to a dull roar inside his ears, and Patrick traced the full curve of Max's lower lip with his thumb.

"Yeah. That." Max tilted his head, resting the weight in Patrick's palm.

God, he loved when Max did that.

"I freaked because you said the exact same words I've been dying to tell you for so long." Max's fingertips dug into the back of Patrick's shirt, holding him tighter against his chest. "I love you so damn much, Patrick Guinness." Max brushed his lips over Patrick's. "Getting you into my arms has been a long, tough battle. But you were a case I was determined to win, big guy."

Damn, his nerd had a way with words. "You mean when I allowed you to win." He grinned.

Max chuckled. "Sure. If you say so."

Epilogue

Max rolled over, savoring the warm feel of Patrick's back against his chest. Patrick stirred and rocked his rear against Max's morning wood. Max sank his teeth into his lower lip, biting back a moan of pleasure.

"Merry Christmas," he whispered.

"Good morning," a raspy, half-asleep voice replied. "And Merry Christmas to you." Patrick turned over and faced him. "You're awake early. You must be eager to see what Santa Claus has brought for you?"

"Very." Max roamed his hand over Patrick's hip and around to a firm buttock. He waggled his eyebrows.

"Hmm… Have you been a good boy?"

"You tell me." He skated his lips over Patrick's. The resulting moan was all the confirmation Max needed.

Breaking away, Max smoothed his palm over Patrick's early morning stubble. "Today is going to be so much fun." He grinned. "Are you looking forward to Christmas dinner with my folks this year?"

"Does a turkey look forward to Thanksgiving?" The

wicked gleam in Patrick's eyes said he was joking.

"Smartass," Max quipped.

"I'm kidding," he drawled. "Actually Liam and I *are* looking forward to this afternoon. I'm sure it'll be fun."

"Dinner is usually a huge spread. Liam will be in heaven." Max laughed.

Ding-dong.

The sound of the doorbell had Max pulling free of Patrick's hold.

"No, you don't," Patrick ordered, reaching out for him. "I'm not finished with you," he growled.

"There's someone at the door." Max pushed his lover's searching hand away from the region of his groin.

"Liam can answer the door." Patrick rose up on his elbows, frowning.

"I want to." Max rolled from the bed, grabbed his robe, and opened the bedroom door. "You coming?"

"I was planning on it, but you seemed to have other ideas."

"You're hysterical, Guinness," Max called out.

By the time he reached the living room, the doorbell was ringing again.

"What the hell, you guys?" Liam said, trudging from his room, his hair covering half his face. "Who's hitting the doorbell this early on Christmas morning? I thought Santa freaking Claus came down the damn chimney."

Max opened the door, and as he'd expected, his present for Liam had arrived by messenger. Getting it delivered on Christmas morning had cost him more money than he wanted to think about. But this was so going to be worth every penny. He tipped the deliveryman generously, then lifted the heavy box from the porch and placed it near their Christmas tree.

Carrying a steaming hot cup of coffee, Patrick strolled from the kitchen in a pair of loose-fitting jogging pants, his chest bare. The man was still the hottest damn thing Max had ever seen. He loved the confidence in his step, the easy, sexy way his hips rocked when he walked. Mentally, he shook his head. He had to look elsewhere or end up aroused and embarrassed in front of the Christmas tree.

He still couldn't believe they were all living together in Patrick's family home, and it was working—much to his sister's delight because, since she was sticking around for school, she'd called dibs on his place. Liam had started his senior year in August, and from what he could tell, the kid had lowered his walls where Max was concerned, and his fears over losing Patrick had quieted.

This year couldn't have ended in a better place when it came to the Guinness and Segreti families.

"What the heck is that?" Patrick laughed and pointed his mug in the direction of the big box Max had set near the tree.

Liam poked his head into the room, a thick slice of fruitcake in his hand. The kid never stopped eating. He had no idea how the guy stayed so thin.

"What is what?" Liam stuffed a large bite of the cake into his mouth. His sleepy gaze searched the room, eventually landing on the new present.

"You really eat that stuff?" Max shot the kid a grossed-out look, and lowered himself onto one of the couch's cushions.

"Yeah," Liam said, hitting him back with a perplexed expression. "It's good."

"If you say so." Max shook his head. "Well, if you can tear yourself away from the fruitcake for a minute, the new box that just arrived is yours, and it's waiting to be opened."

"You're kidding me?" Liam's jaw nearly unhinged with excitement.

"Nope." Max grinned. "It's all yours." He wasn't sure who was more eager to have it opened, him or Liam.

Liam plopped the half-eaten slice on the table and practically leaped toward the tree.

Settling onto sofa beside him, Patrick wrapped an arm around Max's waist. "This is really kind of you, counselor."

"The jury may be out on that verdict," Max said. "Wait until you see what it is first."

"Oh, shit," Patrick muttered.

Liam popped the red ribbon wrapped around the box and lifted the lid. "Oh my God!" he cried out. "A puppy?" He scooped the wiggling cream-colored bundle from the package and into his arms. "Patrick!" Liam jumped up, holding the dog tight. "Look! It's a lab." He held the puppy away from his body for a moment, assessing him. "It's a boy!" Liam laughed and hugged the happily whimpering ball of fur.

Patrick leaned into Max. "I can't believe you did this."

"I know I should have asked you first. But my favorite memories growing up were when my sister and I had a dog."

"Thank you so much, Max," Liam said, still cradling the puppy. "I've always wanted a dog." He kissed the mutt on the head. "He's absolutely perfect." The puppy licked Liam's nose. "I already love him."

Liam sat him on the carpet and soon had the little guy running around, chasing after his hand. They were so adorable together. If Max ever had any doubts about the idea, one look at their interaction said it was the right call.

Max wrapped his arm around Patrick's. "Everyone needs someone or something to love," he said.

Patrick's callused fingers gripped Max's chin, turning his head toward him. "You're absolutely right. And I'm so blessed to have found my someone." His lips touched Max's with a featherlight kiss, but the sensation was enough to send his blood rushing through his veins. Max reached up, ready to hold onto him, to deepen the kiss, but Patrick pulled back, leaving him hanging. Max opened his eyes and found Patrick watching him. "But you're the one who gets to clean up after the beast."

"What?" Max gaped at him. "No fair!"

"Who said anything about life being fair, baby?" Patrick grinned, then a burst of laughter erupted from him. "You should see your face."

Liam lay on the floor playing with his new lab, and his and his brother's sounds of joy filled the room. Max's heart swelled, the love inside nearly taking the muscle beyond tolerance. No matter what the rest of the day brought, he had every Christmas present he could ever want or need right there inside that room.

Acknowledgments

To Naima Simone, you are truly the BEST. This book would not have seen the light of day without your continued encouragement and support. I don't know what I'd ever do without you in my life, and I pray I never have to find out.

To Dahlia Rose, you ROCK! Thank you so much for spending your mornings with me and kicking my behind in gear each day in writing challenges. You are simply amazing, and I'm blessed to know you!

To Alycia, a huge thank you for believing in this book and giving me a chance to tell their story. It's been a pleasure to work with you!

To Heather Howland, thank you so much for all your guidance and help with bringing their story to life.

To the Saints and Sinners, the craziest and the most awesome street team! You are such a tremendous bright spot in my day. I'm so grateful for every comment, every share, tweet, post, or words of encouragement. Your friendship and support mean more to me than you'll ever know.

About the Author

Jessica Lee is an EPIC eBook Award winner and international bestselling author of paranormal romance. She lives in the southeastern United States with her husband and son. In her former life, Jessica was a science geek and spent over twenty-five years as a nurse. But after the birth of her son, she left her medical career behind. During that transition, she discovered her passion for writing romance and has never looked back. Jessica Lee is currently published with Entangled Publishing and Resplendence Publishing. Plus she has several self-published titles available.

Discover more New Adult titles from Entangled Embrace...

THE RULE MAKER
a *Rule Breakers* novel by Jennifer Blackwood

Ten Steps to Surviving a New Job:

1. Don't sleep with the client. It'll get you fired. (Sounds easy enough.) 2. Don't blink when new client turns out to be former one-night stand. 3. Don't call same client a jerk for never texting you back. 6. Ignore accelerated heartbeat every time sexy client walks into room. 8. Don't let client's charm wear you down. Be strong. 9. Whatever you do, don't fall for the client. You'll lose more than your job—maybe even your heart.

ENCORE
an *Amplified* novel by Tara Kelly

I lied my way into a band, humiliated them on stage, and got my heart broken by the bassist. Now...we're on tour together. This is the best opportunity we may ever have – and it's already a disaster. We're broke. We can't stop fighting. And being in such close quarters to Sean isn't exactly helping me get over him. Even though we're just friends now, every time our fingers brush or our eyes catch, my heart betrays me. He's the kind of distraction I can't afford to have right now...no matter how much I wish things were different.

SCARDUST
a novel by Suzanne van Rooyen

DEAD ROCK, TEXAS, 2037

Raleigh made a promise to his brother before he died, that he'd scatter his ashes on Mars. His plans are thwarted when a meteor near-misses him in the desert, and in its crater he finds a man with no memory of who he is—but whenever they touch it ignites a memory swap between them. As their minds and worlds collide, reality unravels and Raleigh must face a painful truth, one that could shatter his dreams of finding love, reaching Mars, and fulfilling his brother's last wish.

WOUND TIGHT
a *Made in Jersey* novel by Tessa Bailey

When CEO Renner Bastion walks into a room, everyone keeps their distance. Well, everyone but the sarcastic, tattooed, Boston-bred security guard whose presence has kept Renner in New Jersey longer than intended. As if the unwanted attraction isn't unsettling enough, Renner finds out Milo isn't as unavailable as originally thought. Worse, his protector is looking for lessons in how to seduce another man. Lessons only Renner can give him.

CPSIA information can be obtained
at www.ICGtesting.com
Printed in the USA
BVHW051129060722
641466BV00001B/20